Cadell, Elizabeth
Royal summons.

MAY 9 '73

Royal Summons

Elizabeth Cadell

ROYAL SUMMONS

William Morrow & Company, Inc.
NEW YORK • 1973

Cadell, Elizabeth.
  Royal summons.

  I. Title.
PZ3.C11427Ro3 [PR6005.A225] 823'.9'12 72-109
ISBN 0-688-00008-8

To
Janet Verdi
with love

Royal Summons

CHAPTER

1

From her room in a Paris hotel, Ellen Berg was telephoning to her travelling companion, self-appointed guardian, and distant cousin, Mrs. Saltry—distant in kinship only, since she was occupying the room next door. The conversation varied little from morning to morning, and was designed to maintain the polite fiction that had been established between them soon after their arrival in Europe, two months earlier.

"Good morning, Corinne. How d'you feel about some sight-seeing?"

"I don't want to hold you up, Nell—I'm only just though drinking my coffee. Why don't you go ahead without me, and we'll fix some place to meet for lunch?"

"I'm going to the Louvre. It'll have to be dinner, I guess."

"The Louvre? You were at the Louvre yesterday and the day before that."

"Yes, I was. I'll be there tomorrow and the day after that. It's kind of a big place. I'll call you when I get back, all right?"

Mrs. Saltry agreed that it was all right, and Nell went

down in the elevator reflecting that although the trip wasn't going according to plan, at least the plan had been switched without friction. She knew now that she would rather have come to Europe alone, and she knew that her cousin was regretting having come at all.

They had left America with a definite object in view—to visit for the first time a property, ruined but historic, which Nell owned in England, and of which she had known nothing until a year ago, when her father had died and she had discovered the fact among his papers. She had only recently made up her mind to go and inspect it; when she decided to include in the plan a preliminary tour of France and Italy, Mrs. Saltry had offered to accompany her, pointing out that as an experienced traveller she was peculiarly fitted to guide a young girl on her first tour of Europe.

It was not Mrs. Saltry's first attempt to act as mother to the motherless Nell. A woman in whom shrewdness and sentiment were almost equally blended, she had endeavoured, ever since the death of her third husband, to make her fitness for the maternal role apparent to Nell's father—but in spite of all her efforts, had made no headway with the taciturn and unimpressionable Matthew Berg. A wealthy rancher, he had chosen to remain a widower, and had brought up his only child in his own way—and what, Mrs. Saltry asked her friends, was the result? Had Nell been taught to dress, to use her charm, to make something of that beautiful figure and that long, heavy, honey-toned hair? No. She could ride and she could shoot, and if anybody wanted a steer, she could go right out and rope one, and what was the use of that to a lovely young girl? Motherless from the age of three, growing up with cows, how could she acquire culture? This trip to Europe was just what she needed, and Mrs. Saltry was going along to see that she got the most out of it.

Mrs. Saltry had another, unacknowledged, reason for making the journey. Her son, Jack, had long been in love with Nell. Having proposed to her twice and twice been rejected, he was hoping that the third time would prove lucky—which it wouldn't, his mother told herself, if Nell went over to Europe alone and got herself mixed up with one of those dollar-hunting Europeans.

The trip had begun in Rome, and before the end of the first week, Mrs. Saltry's guidance—and stamina—had given out. Her previous tours of Europe had been made in comfortable coaches with English-speaking guides, relaxed itineraries, and regular stops for meals; she had no hope of keeping up with Nell, who had proved to be a powerhouse on legs. Why, Mrs. Saltry moaned, why did she have to begin tramping every morning and go on tramping until evening, refusing transport and brushing aside guides? Why should a girl with more money than time want to do things the hard way? Why ruin her eyes over guidebooks with dwarf print when she could pay someone to tell her anything she wanted to know? Why wear out her shoes when there were cabs to take her wherever she wanted to go? Would Nell, or anybody else, please tell her why she had been so crazy as to come on this trip?

Nell, watching her limping and looking desperately for the nearest taxi, had at first thought that age was taking its toll—Corinne, she recalled pityingly, was all of fifty. But she found that it was more than age. Where, she wondered, had she ever got the idea that Corinne spoke fluent French and could make herself understood in Italian? How had the townsfolk of Chenco, Arizona—no fools, and many of them seasoned travellers—come to regard her as an authority on European art and culture? Authority? She didn't know Baroque from Byzantine, she couldn't tell Manet from Monet, and she got the Pope mixed up with the Holy Roman Emperor—though, give her her due, she'd recognized the Eiffel Tower right away. But why come at all, if all she'd wanted was to hole up in the nearest Hilton and do her sight-seeing in beauty parlours and boutiques?

The team of two had separated. Since then, both had been

happy. Nell was hungry for knowledge and her hunger was being satisfied. Mrs. Saltry travelled in taxis round the shopping districts, and to complete her satisfaction, had several times discovered, behind American newspapers in hotel lounges, gentlemen temporarily or permanently separated from their wives, only too willing to take the place of the middle-aged or elderly admirers and escorts whom she had left behind in Chenco and missed so much.

But she was becoming restless. They had come, she reminded herself, to see this house of Nell's—so when were they going to get to it? Rome, Florence, Venice, Paris—for heaven's sake, how many more pictures, how many more galleries and statues and dates and facts could Nell take in? For herself, all she wanted was to see this house in England and then go back home. She had been a fool to say out loud, before they started, that time was no object. She ought to have set a time limit. Enough was enough.

When she was ready for dinner that evening, she went to Nell's room. Nell, enveloped in an enormous bath towel, waved her to a chair and brought her a drink from the refrigerator-disguised-as-antique-cabinet.

"Thank you." Mrs. Saltry took the glass. "Did you have a nice day?"

"Marvellous. Greek and Roman antiquities day. Augur consulting the entrails of a bull in front of the temple of Jupiter in . . ."

Mrs. Saltry shuddered. "Will you please save it till I've had dinner?"

"Sorry." Nell was pulling on a dress. "How can anyone get their minds back to thousands of years before Christ? Listen to this, for instance: quote, 'Stele dedicated by Queen Hatshepsut to her father, Thothmes, fifteen thirty to fifteen twenty B.C.,' end of quote. From Hattie to Thomas, with love. Did you know that one of the things they used in Egyptian ceremonies—an essential offering, the guidebook said —was the rear hoof of an ox?"

"No, I did *not* know. Is that what you came all the way over here to find out? Come over here and I'll fix that zipper. We're going to have dinner at a little restaurant in the Place St. Michel. Oh, and we'll be three."

Nell turned from the dressing table. "Three?"

"Yes."

"Who's the third?"

"I was sitting in the hotel lobby waiting for the porter to call me a cab, when—"

"Not again?" Nell moaned. "Oh, Corinne, can't you wait till you get home? You've got all the men friends you want in Chenco—why do you have to talk to strangers and—"

"Nell, I do *not* talk to strangers. But as I've tried to explain to you, if you have a man with you when you go to a restaurant, you get better service."

"What's so hard about ordering a meal?"

"Without an escort, you know what happens. The waiters pretend you're not there. You get pushed to a table off in a corner. Now, with Mr. Slasenger, we—"

"Who?"

"He's that nice, gray-haired—"

"I wish you wouldn't pick up people."

"I do not pick up people. When I'm so far from home, I think it's silly to sit beside a quiet, nicely behaved gentleman I know is an American, and not say a single word. I think it's right we should talk to fellow Americans."

"You mean American fellows. I feel kind of sorry for them, Corinne. I know it's a social and not a sexual gap you're filling, but they don't know—until they find out. How do I look?"

"You're a very lovely girl."

"Thank you. I know. But the dress?"

Mrs. Saltry finished her drink and rose with a sigh. "You'll never make the top ten, Nell."

"Too bad. Let's go. I bet this old Mr. What's-his-name is getting ready to make a proposition."

Mr. Slasenger would have had to shout it aloud—the restaurant was crowded and the noise deafening—but it was more likely to have remained unspoken under Nell's direct, candid gaze, which told him clearly that she considered him too old to be dangerous. He passed the evening enjoying the contrast between his two companions. The younger one, he thought, looked as fresh as spring, but he decided that if he had not been a happily married man, he would have gone for the older one—she had a kind of finish, a gloss, with her small, slim body, close-fitting, elegant dress, and smooth little chestnut head.

He drove them back to the hotel. On the way they learned that he was soon going over to England to meet his wife, who was coming from America to join him for their fiftieth wedding anniversary. He received their congratulations with pleasure, saw them safely inside the hotel, and departed.

"Now, you can't say he wasn't nice, can you?" Mrs. Saltry demanded.

Nell gave a great yawn. "Bed," she said longingly. "Are you coming with me tomorrow?"

"No. I'm shopping. So would you if you had any sense. You haven't been inside a store since you left home. Come up to my room, Nell. I ordered some lemon tea—for you, too. It'll do you good."

Nell refused the tea, and was going to say good night when something in the older woman's manner checked her. "Homesick?" she asked.

"Yes and no."

Nell followed her into her room. "If not homesick, then what?"

"I don't know what. Sit down. Look, could we set a day for going to England?"

"Where's the hurry? Aren't you happy here?"

"I'm comfortable, if that's what you mean. But don't you think you've done enough sight-seeing for one trip? There's still all London to look at. It's been two months, and here's

June already, and what we really came for, in case you don't remember, was to take a look at that house of yours. You did write to that lawyer, didn't you? What was his name?"

"Brierley. No, I didn't."

"You *didn't?* Oh, Nell, you were going to write to him from Venice!"

"I forgot. I'll write in the morning and tell him we're on our way."

"And don't forget to ask him if the old lady's still alive."

"How could she be, Corinne? She'd be a hundred years old, if not two hundred."

"When I read those letters you found after your father died, I figured she was only fifteen years older than your mother. If your mother had lived, she'd be only fifty-seven. Add fifteen to that, and you get . . . what do you get?"

"Seventy-two."

"So that's not two hundred, and she might still be alive, and if she is, she's your great-aunt and she ought to be told you're coming."

"If she's alive, the lawyer'll tell her. How do we know the lawyer's alive?"

"It wouldn't matter if he was dead—his office would still go on. There's never only one of those lawyers. They'll be Brierley, Brierley, Brierley, and Brierley. One takes up where the other leaves off. Can't you ask him to write to this address?"

"Why can't I just say we'll show up—sometime?"

Mrs. Saltry made an impatient sound and poured herself some lemon tea. "I don't understand you anymore, Nell. Now that you're so near, don't you feel the least bit of excitement about seeing the place?"

"Not as much as when I left home. Maybe we should have started there and left all this"—her gesture took in all the ground they had covered—"until after." She paused to study her cousin's face. "I hate leaving here, but I guess we have to. You've had just about enough, haven't you?"

"I'm happy to stay as long as you want me to," lied Mrs. Saltry. "But what I think is, it's time you got to England. I just said I didn't understand you, and that's true—I don't. How could anyone? When I went to stay at the ranch after your father died, you'd just finished reading all those old letters about this house in England, and you were all worked up and—"

"Wouldn't you have been, in my place? If you'd gone through your whole life believing there was nothing you couldn't discuss with your father, no secrets anywhere, everything out in clear daylight—and then you found he hadn't even told you who your mother really was, and that she owned this manor house and when she died it was yours—I mean mine—and it had been there all those years and he'd never said a word about it—well, you'd feel kind of strange, wouldn't you? Not a word to me, to—"

"To anyone. That shouldn't surprise you. If there was a man in this world with a bigger talent for keeping his mouth shut than your father, I have yet to meet him. When I was little, and used to visit at the ranch, he'd go whole days without saying one word to me, or to my mother and father. It wasn't that he didn't like us; he just didn't talk. How he kept his mouth open long enough to ask your mother to marry him I shall never know. Maybe she sensed what he was after. But when I read those letters, Nell, I told you what I thought, and I still think it: he didn't tell you anything about where your mother had come from, and who she'd been, because he was scared you'd do what she did, only the other way round."

"You mean he thought I'd want to go and live in England? I don't believe it."

"Try figuring it out. You were his only child, and he'd got that ranch spreading over half of Arizona, and a few million dollars to hand down—so what would you have done in his place? Tell you your mother had been Lady Helen Stapling, daughter of the last earl of I forget what, and that when she died, you became the owner of this I forget how many centuries-old house?"

"Not a house—a ruin."

"All right—ruin. Try to see it his way. If he had told you while you were still a child, maybe you'd have grown up with a lot of fancy ideas. If he'd told you when you were maybe eighteen or nineteen, you might have got ideas about going off to see the place, and how did he know you'd come back? Your mother never went back to her home. All he wanted—"

"I know what he wanted." For a moment her voice faltered. "I keep remembering how much he wanted it. He wanted me to marry a rancher and settle down on the ranch forever. He was always lining up all those young men, hoping I'd choose one."

"My son Jack among them."

"Yes. And you know that Jack was the only one I came near to marrying, and I'm sorry I wasn't in love with him enough so's I could marry him and make everybody, my father and you and Jack and myself, happy. I think the first thing I liked, really liked, about you was the way you didn't hold it against me."

"Mothers never hold that against a girl. They look at their son and they figure that the girl could never find anyone better and is out of her mind not to snatch him while she can get him. Which I hope you will. But don't let's get off the point. The point is that when you read all those letters of your mother's, and the lawyer's, you made up your mind you'd come over to England and inspect your house or ruin. And now you're near it, and the nearer you get, the more reasons you think up for not getting any nearer. So explain. What exactly do you want to do?"

Nell, who had refused lemon tea, now poured herself a cup, stared at it absently, and left it untouched. She lay on the bed, clasped her hands behind her head and spoke, staring up at the ceiling. "I don't know what I want to do,

Corinne. I only know what I don't want to do. I don't want to go home before I've taken in enough of what I'm taking in now to last me a long, long time—maybe all the rest of my life. I can't get the hang of all the pictures and the statues and the architecture. I try, but I don't get the *feel*. But history . . . that's different. It's suddenly come alive. All those dreary dates, all those dead kings and queens"—she sat up and gazed at Mrs. Saltry—"they're not dates, they're not names anymore. They're alive. They're *here*. They walked up those stairs, they looked out of those windows, they were cheered in that place and had their heads cut off in another. I feel . . . I don't know how I feel. Kind of drunk."

"If you'd wanted to come to Europe with your father," Mrs. Saltry began, "he would have . . ." She broke off, and Nell smiled.

"Would have? You know very well it took a world war to get him off the ranch, and it would have taken another world war to make him move off it again. The ranch was his life, his . . . well, I don't have to tell you."

"No. You don't."

Nell made a restless movement. "You know something that still puzzles me, something I still can't figure out? How was it that nobody ever found out that my mother wasn't just plain Mrs. Matthew Berg? How was it that none of my father's old wartime buddies, the ones who'd been with him in England when he met my mother—how come they never showed up and said, 'Why, if it isn't old Matt and Lady Helen'? Why?"

"Because America's a big place. Bigger than the Louvre even. Take a group of G.I.'s cut out of the main body and sent to this little place called—what was it called?"

"Rivering."

"Rivering. There wouldn't have been all that many of them, and your father was never the buddy type. Bring them back to America and spread them out, and you'll find most of them are a long, long way from the ranch. And because your father would have drowned himself sooner than go to any of those reunions or get-togethers or old-comrade rackets, you can see that plain Mrs. Matthew could have become a natural part of the Arizona landscape. And you only have to read those letters to know that she wasn't interested in going back to visit her old home."

"All she said was she wouldn't go back while her aunt was alive."

"If she'd really wanted to go home, she wouldn't have cared whether there was an old aunt in it or not. Now I come to think of it, if her aunt had died, somebody would have written to say so. I don't mind betting you'll find she's still around, making life hell for everybody the way your mother said she did. Is that why you're putting off getting there?"

"No. It's just that there's so much to see on the way, so much to learn, so much to take in."

"Well, keep working at it—only don't forget you've got a home waiting for you in America, and a fine young man, and a life that fifty million girls would give their—"

"Did my mother talk much about England?"

"If the subject ever came up, and I was the only one who ever brought it up, she'd answer questions. I got to know how your father had been sent to this place—don't tell me—Rivering, and how they fell in love but there was this old aunt who tried to stop them, and how they got married just the same and your mother went to the ranch when the war was over and never left it again. But not one word, ever, about last earls or historic houses or titles."

"When I read those letters," Nell said slowly, "the first thing I couldn't understand was why, if my father didn't want me to know anything about what was in them, he didn't burn the evidence. Why didn't he?"

"Because it would have been dishonest, that's why, and so he couldn't have made himself do it. Besides that, he knew there'd have to be more letters one day, saying the old lady had got herself murdered, or asking why you don't put the ruin on the market. Which is what I advise you to do before we go back home—unless you're figuring on rebuilding it."

"Rebuilding it?" Nell echoed in astonishment. "Why should I want to rebuild it? I don't want to live in England."

"I'm glad to know it. Some people have to, but that's their problem. I'd like to stay out of it."

"But your—"

"—second husband was an Englishman. That's why I know what I'm talking about. It didn't last a year, but it felt like ten."

"But you told everybody in Chenco—"

"I know what I told everybody in Chenco, and it was all true, the part about the state dining room and the deer park. All I didn't say was that the temperature of the house was forty below zero and it was four miles from the kitchens to the state dining room, and the only way I knew my husband was still alive was if I heard hounds baying or guns going off, or if they served salmon for dinner. I tried getting to know the neighbours, only ten miles off in any direction, but all they ever used for conversation was 'Oh, really?' "

"Well, it was a long time ago, and I only know what my father told me . . ."

"And your father only knew what I told him, which wasn't much, and he advised me to marry Red Saltry, so I did, and I was happy because when I wanted him, there he was, right beside me, not striding over the heather miles away. When he died, I could have married again, but I didn't. The only man I wanted was your father, and he pretended he didn't know what I was after. How did we get onto husbands? I could go on all night. Let's get back to what I said in the first place: when do we leave here?"

Nell rose and walked to the door. "Any day you like," she said. "You name it."

"Do you mean that?"

"Yes. I'd like to spend some time in London first, if that's all right with you."

"London I can take. Just keep me off those moors, that's all. Wait a minute while I write down the name of that place."

"Rivering."

"That wasn't the name of the house, was it?"

"No. The house is called Stapling Manor."

"I get it. Same as the last earl."

"No. The earls were the earls of Bosfield."

"Then I don't get it."

"It's easy if you put your mind to it. Stapling Manor is on a hill above a town called Rivering. The manor was the home of the Staplings. A Stapling got to be earl of Bosfield. That's all I know until I get to see that lawyer and ask him some questions."

"I can wait. Tomorrow, Nell, I'll see about making hotel reservations in London. Say Thursday?"

"Suits me," Nell said. "Good night."

CHAPTER

2

It was such a perfect morning that Mr. Brierley decided to walk to work. The unprecedented warmth which met him as he stepped out of the house prompted him to go inside again to look for his light-weight jacket, which after a prolonged search he found hanging behind his windbreaker in the closet. Putting it on, he glanced at himself in the hall mirror; it was badly creased, but he hoped that nobody would notice. He went out again, a tall, thin, stooping, still handsome, timid, painfully shy old man, and crossed the dusty lane that separated the house from the pinewood growing on the hillside.

He seldom walked to his office; when he did, he took the path through the woods, dropping down to the open, windy heath and skirting it to reach the busy market town of Rivering—but as a rule he went in his old two-seater car down the winding road that led eventually to the market square. It was a road little used, for on this side of the hill there were only three houses—his own, and one of similar size and design on each side of it.

He turned to make sure he had closed the front door; sometimes he forgot, and came home in the evening to find that the wind had played havoc with his possessions. But the door was closed, as were the front doors of the other two houses. The three were small, square, stone-built, their backs forming part of the beautiful old wall of Stapling Manor. From where he stood, Cosmo could see the high wrought-iron gate which gave entrance to the manor grounds from this side; over the wall he could see the tops of trees gently waving. The rest was dusty lane and pinewood and peace.

His eyes rested for a few moments on the house he occupied. He saw that the curtains hung badly and were not as clean as they should be. He knew that behind the curtains there were carpets which had not been swept, dishes which had not been washed, litter lying on every table and chair. Not a home to be proud of, he acknowledged to himself, but all the same, a home in which he was very . . .

He checked the conclusion sharply and turned into the cool wood. A squirrel darted across his path, and he remembered that in the not-so-very-distant past he had liked to pretend that he was a squirrel, lively and springy—and free. He had spent a good deal of his time pretending. Sometimes he had pretended not to be there at all—that had helped. What had helped most of all was pretending that he wasn't married.

He grew chilly at the disloyalty of the thought. She had been such a good wife. Look at the persistence with which she had tried to make something of him. She had found him a shabby solicitor in a seedy office, and she had married him, smartened him up, made him rent the house on the hill, and kept it like a bandbox—shining floors, gleaming furniture, polished silver—how pretty it had looked, and how upset she had become if anything got out of place. He had pretended sometimes that they had a dozen children, strong children who would help him to mow or weed or sweep or wash dishes—but he had given up that particular pretense because it struck him as a poor life to offer children.

He sighed—a happy sigh. It was a beautiful June morning, and he didn't feel anywhere near his age, and it was wonderful to be done with pretending. All that puzzled him nowadays was how a man who had lived in a house so immaculate could be so happy in . . . There. The word was out. Happy. Why deny it? He was happy, and he was happy because he was no longer compelled to spend his leisure hours doing housework.

When his wife had died, ten years ago, he had done his best to go on keeping things tidy, but he had created disorder faster than he could clear it up, so he had ceased to clear it up and he had begun to be happy, as he had been in his bachelor days. He was happy because there were no more lists of tasks which his wife ticked off as he finished them, no more admonitions to be quicker or more thorough. He was happy because he had round him once again all the things that made his life so pleasant and comfortable—his books, his newspapers, his chessmen and packs of patience cards, his sketching block and old felt slippers and packets of cough lozenges, his little wireless set and his four clocks, three of which wouldn't go. Everything round him—nothing tidied away, hidden away, swept away—everything ready at hand, everything waiting, like good servants, to be called upon.

He had reached the center of the town and he remembered with the feeling of guilt that invariably accompanied memories of his wife, that it was to this square—the market square —that she had planned to move his office, here among the successful professional men. But the move had never been made. He still had to turn off into a narrow side street—his wife had said that its downward slope was symbolic—and make his way along streets even narrower and meaner, until he came to the cul-de-sac in which, squeezed between the commercial school and the Youth Club, was his down-at-heel office, with its incongruous, gleaming brass plate: *Cosmo Brierley. Solicitor*. It was the only plate he now cleaned, and he kept it shining because it was his sole source of pride. There were other Brierleys in the town, but there was only one Cosmo. He often wondered if it was the Cosmo that had made his wife decide to give up her flourishing commercial school in order to marry him.

He went up four steps and entered the damp-smelling passage. His rooms were on the right, opposite *Veal Bros., Jobbing Gardeners, Telephone 576.882, ring before 8 a.m.* On the dun-coloured, peeling wall, a faded arrow pointed to a notice halfway up the stairs: *Miss Una Dell. Dressmaker. By appointment only*.

He entered his outer office. From behind a desk littered with cuttings of dress material, an angular figure rose to give him formal greeting.

"Good morning, Mr. Brierley."

"Good morning, Miss Dell."

"You're not as early as usual." Miss Dell's voice was low-pitched, her accent and bearing exceedingly refined. "I hope the car didn't have a puncture?"

"No. I didn't use the car today. I walked, as it was such a lovely morning."

"Indeed, yes." Miss Dell inclined her head and resumed her seat. "As there was nothing pressing this morning, I thought you wouldn't mind my looking through these samples of material."

"Of course not." Cosmo hung his drooping Panama on the hatstand in a corner and opened the door of his own room. It looked just as he had left it the evening before—dusty, disorderly, his home away from home, as it used to be in the carefree days before the commercial school had opened next door. No, not quite the same, for in those days there had been nobody in the outer office.

(25)

He would have found it difficult to explain exactly how Miss Una Dell had come to work as his part-time secretary. He could not remember making the suggestion to her; all he knew was that once, in the dim past, there had been three Misses Dell living and working with their mother in the rooms above his office. Mrs. Dell and two misses had died, and the trickle of clients making their way up the creaky stairs had dwindled and finally ceased, and he had sat in his office listening uneasily to the scufflings that told him that Una, the last Miss Dell, was preparing her meager lunch, or her tea, and he had wondered how she could manage to exist on the pittance which, as her lawyer, he knew was all she possessed. Somehow she had materialized in his outer office, and his fear that she would set about tidying it up died when he discovered that she did not even realize that it needed tidying.

Her duties, such as they were, she took seriously, receiving his few clients with dignity and doing her best to give an impression of clerkly efficiency. She certainly looked impressive; she had fine, brown eyes, a crown of gray plaits, well-curved lips and a nose that would have added importance to a Roman proconsul. Unfortunately, her wits were beginning to wander, and Cosmo was asked with increasing frequency why he continued to employ her. He had no reply to give, the truth being that the more odd she became, the more responsible he felt for her.

At noon every day, she left the office—to do her shopping, she said, but Cosmo knew that she went to fill not her string bag but her gossip-loving mind. Gray-suited, gray-gloved, gray-hatted, picture of a dead past, she went from shop to shop, propping her bicycle outside and going in to absorb news items which she took back to people her lonely evenings. Each morning, on Cosmo's arrival at the office, she gave him an edited version of the gossip.

"They found Mrs. Brown's handbag," she told him now. "Where do you think it was? Just where she said she had left it—in the bus. But it had gotten wedged behind the seat. A small boy found it when he was fidgeting about, and the conductor gave it back to Mrs. Brown. Lucky, wasn't it?"

Cosmo made his usual effort to appear interested. "Yes, indeed. Is there any post?"

"That girl, Mary Battley, has had her baby. She's going to call it Cora—that's the grandmother's name. But she refuses to have it adopted. Do you think she's right?"

"Well, I can't really . . ."

"In my opinion, she's doing the right thing. She's gone back to London and she's left the baby with her sister—the sister who's a nurse. They say she's left plenty of money for its keep."

"Good. Were there any letters?"

"Ah, I was just coming to that. I got a letter this morning telling me that the rent of my rooms is to be put up. That means that the rent of this office will go up too. In fact, I remember now—there's a letter to that effect in your mail."

"I was expecting something of the kind," Cosmo said. "They want to get us out, of course. They want to sell the building, but nobody will buy it until we go."

"I know. We're what they call sitting tenants, aren't we? If they did turn us out, you'd have your nice little house to go to, but I should find myself in rather a difficulty."

"They can't turn us out. May I see the letter?"

"Certainly. I had it here only a moment ago." Miss Dell began to rummage among some papers at the side of her desk, and then paused. "Oh, there's a large notice outside the hotel saying it's going to open next week. That's to say, re-open. They say it's completely renovated, new dining room, new kitchens, snack bar, and even bathrooms added to some of the bedrooms. I wouldn't have said we needed anything of that sort in Rivering, but they tell me the place is fully booked for months ahead. It's going to be very hard on the White Hart."

"I don't think I agree," Cosmo said mildly. "The people

who go to the White Hart are mostly farmers, and farmers don't want snack bars. They want good, solid food, which is what the White Hart gives them. They . . ."

He stopped. Miss Dell, gathering up her snippets of material, had dislodged the sheaf of papers. They fluttered to the floor, and Cosmo stooped to pick them up.

"The letter isn't among these," he said.

"Letter?"

"The letter you mentioned, the one about—"

"Oh, of course! How silly of me. You say it isn't with those papers?"

"No."

"Not?"

"No."

"In that case, perhaps I put it into a drawer." She pulled out several, revealing half-finished lengths of knitting, out-of-date pattern books, two faded velvet pincushions and several skeins of wool. "No, I don't see it. Would you oblige me by seeing if I put it on your desk?"

He obliged her and reported that there was no letter there.

"Never mind," Miss Dell said tranquilly. "It'll come to light later, I expect. I must have put it with the other letter. I took the stamp off the envelope—I hope you don't mind?"

"No, I don't mind at all, but the letter—"

"I remember now. There were two letters only. They . . . could they have slipped under my chair? No. Never mind. I shall go on looking and bring them to you when they turn up. One of them, as I told you, was about the rent going up. It was the other one which had the French stamp."

Cosmo paused on his way into his room. "French?"

"Yes. I opened it. You did instruct me, did you not, to open all correspondence that was not marked *Personal?*"

"Yes. Was this letter . . ."

"It was nothing important." Miss Dell rose from a further search on the floor and shook the dust off her skirt, and the particles rose in a fog that seemed to Cosmo a symbol of the uneasiness that was beginning to cloud his mind. "You know, Mr. Brierley, it often strikes me that we ought to have a filing system but we need a filing cabinet or something of that kind."

"A good idea," he said absently. "I shall order one. Was the letter . . ."

"The stamp was French. But the writer was an American."

Cosmo's hand closed tightly round the handle of his door. "American?"

"Yes. Where *could* I have . . . ah!" With a cry of triumph, Miss Dell leaned across and twitched a letter from behind the clock on the mantelpiece. "Here it is! I noticed that the clock was losing, and went to put it right, and I must have . . . yes, that was it. Here it is."

She held it out, and Cosmo took it, but his eyes remained on Miss Dell. "American?" he repeated.

"Yes. But nothing important. I merely glanced at it and saw that it was another of those people wanting to come and see the Manor."

Her voice held the strained note that always sounded when she had occasion to mention Stapling Manor but Cosmo had ceased to listen. With the letter in his hand, he walked slowly into his room and closed the door. He sat down on his swivel chair and drew the single sheet from the envelope and looked at the signature. Then he got up again. He would take the blow—and blow he knew it would be— on his feet.

The writing covered both sides of the sheet of paper. On first reading, there seemed to be nothing that could alarm him, and he reproached himself for being too easily frightened. When he read the letter a second time, however, his mind began to take in its dreadful possibilities. Without knowing what he was doing, he crushed the paper into his jacket pocket and went to stare sightlessly out of the window.

It had come, as he had known it must. Known? No, he hadn't known; he had only feared. Long ago, he had voiced his fears—many times, and with all his force, if it could be called force. He had made no impression whatsoever. She had made plan after plan, and she had carried each into execution. She had brushed aside his protests, and at last he had ceased to make any, comforting himself with the thought that he would in all probability be dead and gone before the hour of reckoning came. But it had come, and he wasn't dead and he hadn't gone, and however convincingly he might argue, to himself and to others, that the fault was not his, the responsibility would be placed squarely at his door. He had been appointed trustee, sole trustee, and he had allowed himself to be overridden. Worse: as the years went by, he had allowed himself to turn a blind eye. And now . . .

His hand felt for the letter in his pocket, but he did not need to read it again; he knew its contents by heart. He felt an urge to go home, to walk up the hill again and try to assess the full measure of the disaster.

He went back to the outer office and took down his hat, and Miss Dell looked at him in surprise.

"Have you an appointment in the town?" she inquired.

"No. That is . . . no. As a matter of fact, I have to go back to the house."

She looked at him more closely. "I would advise you not to walk up that steep hill," she said. "You look rather pale. You should go up in a taxi."

But it was on his feet that he made the journey through the wood, walking slowly over the carpet of pine needles, staring at the ground and letting his mind wander over the past. It was seldom that he cared to recall it, much less dwell on it—but now it was in his pocket and it was no longer the past, but the future. The immediate future.

Halfway up the hill, he paused and looked down through the trees. From here he could see spread out the town and its surroundings. The river made a loop round the town, isolating it, leaving only a bottleneck through which, since there were no bridges across the river, all incoming and outgoing traffic had to pass. There was no railway link, and frequent flooding of the river made the bottleneck impassable for many days in the spring and autumn. It was the floods which had made the soil so rich and so productive. Rivering produce was famous and Rivering farmers were rich, but they remained farmers, adding to their acres but refusing to widen their mental outlook, content with their ancient market square and their two ugly churches, and presenting to any proposed changes so adamantine a front that progressive sons and daughters took their ideas elsewhere.

But Cosmo had not paused in order to look at the town. The point at which he was standing was by tradition the demarcation line between Rivering and Stapling. Below was the town; on the plateau above was Stapling Manor, the centuries-old house with its surrounding wall, its moat, its mausoleum with the tiny adjoining chapel, its ancient bridge and—beyond the wall on one side—the three modern stone houses; on the other side, some acres of heath and woodland were all that remained of the Manor's once-extensive domain. The main entrance to the grounds was by the wide, gradually-ascending road from the town which ended in a beautiful, mile-long beech avenue.

Cosmo, walking on with dragging steps up to his house, attempted to find solace in his old habit of pretense, to remove himself in spirit to a faraway place where no news of the Manor could reach him—but no pretending could remove the letter from his pocket. There could be no pretense, no escape; he was about to be called to account.

He was at the gate of his house, about to open it, when he heard the sound of rhythmic, rubber-shod footsteps. He did not have to turn in order to identify the sound; it was his neighbour, Mr. Moulton, returning from his morning exercise, which took the form of a sharp trot round the perimeter of the Manor. Seeing Cosmo, he stopped beside him, but his legs continued to work like pistons. He was large and stout and florid; he was wearing a vest and running shorts. Both were sweat-stained, and his full cheeks glistened.

"Morning, Brierley," he puffed. "Taken a day off?"

"No. I went down to the office this morning, but I . . . I came back."

"So I see. You look . . . a bit . . . pasty. Out of sorts?"

"No, oh, no, thank you. I'm quite well."

"You don't look it. You didn't . . . run into Lady Laura . . . by any chance?"

Cosmo flushed. He was aware that the Moultons despised him for being afraid of an old woman but they had nothing to do with her, he reflected, apart from paying their rent regularly. They weren't trustees who had to answer for . . .

"No," he answered Mr. Moulton, and watched him trot to his own gate, up the neat path and into his house. There was relief in his eyes, but there was also a certain wistfulness. He would have liked to talk to someone—anyone. Anyone but Mr. Moulton, who might have listened sympathetically, but whose encouragement took the form of hearty back-slapping and vigorous pokes in the ribs. Himself perennially free from care, Mr. Moulton found it difficult to follow the reasoning of those who took life more seriously.

Mr. and Mrs. Moulton had been the first to rent one of the houses on the hill. They were then in their late thirties; they had taken a lease of a few months only, since at the end of that time Mr. Moulton's period of leave would expire and they would return to his official post in British India. Unfortunately, British India had expired first, and the Moultons had found themselves stranded in Stapling. Mrs. Moulton had bitterly lamented the severance from Rajahs and Residencies, but it would have taken more than the decline of an empire to dampen Mr. Moulton's spirits. Robbed of the hope of ending his days under a plumed topee, he decided to seek success in business, and began by renting the disused stables of the Manor, establishing a riding school and putting it under the direction of his wife. He himself presided over his second venture: the Simon Moulton Bridge School which, to the consternation of the local husbands, had proved an instant and brilliant success—the women of Rivering and the surrounding districts seemed to have been waiting for a Simon Moulton. They turned eagerly from bingo to bridge, and were still playing. To the spacious bridge rooms Mr. Moulton later added a snack bar, which did a steady business.

There had been a kind of frosty friendliness between Mrs. Moulton and Cosmo's wife, and on the latter's death, Mrs. Moulton had gone to some trouble to engage daily women to keep his house in order. But one after another had stated the task to be beyond them, and when the fifth resigned, Mrs. Moulton told Cosmo sharply that if he wished to live in a pigsty, there was nothing more she could do about it. Her own house was as orderly as Cosmo's had been during the ten years of his marriage, for she and her husband were seldom in it; Mr. Moulton made curries for himself in the snack bar; Mrs. Moulton lived on yogurt and fruit.

Cosmo, about to go into his house, changed his mind and walked slowly along the road to the great iron gate. He used his key to open it, locked it behind him and went on in the direction of the lake, head bent, his mind on the letter he carried in his pocket. Raising his head, he saw some distance away the summerhouse with its beautiful saddleback roof; beside it shimmered the lake, and reflected in the water were the banks of flowers grown for marketing. Beyond the woodland that surrounded the lake he could see the chimneys of the Manor house.

He stopped, his eyes on the summerhouse. It was separated from the lake by a wide, natural terrace, and on the terrace he saw something which in the past month or two had become a familiar sight: a fringed hammock slung between two trees on the lake's edge. On the hammock, slowly swinging, lay a large, powerfully-built man of about thirty. His eyes were closed and he looked asleep, but Cosmo knew better than to approach him; it had been made clear to him, and to others, that when Hallam Grant looked asleep, he was doing his best work.

He had come to Stapling only four months ago, having rented the third of the stone houses—the one next door to the Moultons'. In addition to renting this, he had to Cosmo's surprise also rented the summerhouse, long disused. He had had it repaired and had then furnished it—sparsely, but adequately—and now spent most of his time in it, or in the hammock, or at his typewriter on a table on the terrace. Cosmo had assumed that he was a writer, but had learned that he was by profession an archaeologist, in Stapling only to revise a book he had written on the subject. Writing or revising, he had demanded the same conditions of peace and privacy; he did not welcome interruptions.

Cosmo walked reluctantly on. Talking to Grant would have helped. Young as he was, he had an outlook which Cosmo recognized as more adult than his own. But he was asleep, or working, or both.

Hallam Grant opened one eye and studied the retreating back. There went the old boy, looking more cowed than usual. What was it about that old woman that could put the fear of God into anybody? Yet every time the two met, Cosmo lost another ounce or two. What was it like to go through life being walked over?

He obeyed an impulse, and called. "Hello, Cosmo."

Cosmo turned and came eagerly back. "Good morning. I thought . . . that's to say, you were asleep. I hope I didn't disturb you?"

Hallam did not answer this; he had a habit of leaving

questions unanswered from time to time. If only, Cosmo thought yearningly, if only he could have found the courage to do that when his wife was alive.

"Sit down and have a drink," Hallam invited.

There was nothing to sit on, and no sign of anything to drink. Cosmo waited, watching the other man give a long yawn, a prolonged stretch and finally a roll which brought him out of the hammock onto his feet.

"You get the chair, I'll get the drinks," Hallam directed. "No, not that chair. The one with the cushions."

Cosmo placed the chair in the dappled shade, sat down, leaned back and gazed across the lake. A lovely setting, he mused. Odd that nobody had ever thought before of doing what this man had done—renting the empty summerhouse and making it into a kind of retreat. Where could there be a spot more peaceful, more beautiful?

"Here you are." Hallam came out holding two glasses. Under his arm was a folding table which Cosmo rose to unfold and place between the chair and the hammock. "You look as though you need a drink. Has the old lady been bullying you again?"

"Oh, no indeed. I—"

"Why don't you settle down and have lunch with me? Or do you have to go to the office?"

"No. I went down this morning, and then came back. Please don't bother about lunch for me. I can easily—"

"We'll have it together, out here. I've got cheese and pâté and biscuits—and some nice Rivering tomatoes, big and red and ripe."

Cosmo sipped his drink. He did not want to eat or drink, but as he leaned against the cushions, he felt the morning's fear and tension draining out of him, and felt grateful. And envious. So near to the Manor, this young man was nevertheless free, unafraid, detached. He lived here, but he was uninterested in, untroubled by the Manor and its past, and

—incredibly—indifferent to anything that Lady Laura might say or do.

Hallam had settled himself once more in the hammock. "Drink all right?" he asked.

"It's very nice indeed, thank you. Perhaps a little, er, strong?"

"Tell me," Hallam said, "what's worrying you?"

"Oh, there's nothing that—"

"Yes, there is. I suppose Lady Laura's been at you again. What is it," he asked curiously, "that makes you so frightened of that woman? I know she hisses, but she doesn't actually bite. How can you, after a lifetime of her, still find her formidable?"

Cosmo took a deep draught and spoke slowly. "I'm not— at least, I don't think I am—afraid of her," he said. "It's . . . well, it's the things she does. Things she has no possible right to do. As her lawyer and as trustee of this estate, I try to stop her—that is, I used to try to stop her—from doing the things I knew to be wrong, illegal. I found it was no use. If I appear frightened, it's because—"

"Because you'll get blamed, is that it?"

This was so exactly it that Cosmo found himself without a reply. His eyes went instinctively to the Manor, and Hallam spoke reassuringly.

"Stop worrying. She won't come this way."

"No, probably not. It's getting near lunch time, and . . ."

"She won't come this way again. I made it clear, this morning, that if she wants to go to and from the Manor, she's got to go by the road on the other side of the lake. I made that a condition when I rented the summerhouse, but she either forgot, or chose to ignore it. Today, I made sure she wouldn't forget again."

Cosmo spoke earnestly. "But that's just the difficulty with Lady Laura," he said. "She disregards any wishes but her own. You haven't been here long enough to realize that ask-

(36)

ing, telling, even begging her is no use at all. She takes absolutely no notice. None. From the day her niece went away, all those years ago, she has been . . . well, uncontrollable. I am not speaking of my own efforts only. I admit that I have not been strong enough to stand up to her—but others, much stronger than I am, have insisted, have protested, and nothing has moved her. Nothing has prevented her from getting what she wanted. The fact that you object to her going past this summerhouse will, I promise you, make no difference at all. She will still . . ."

"No, she won't. She went past this morning for the last time—the last, that is, during my tenancy. I warned her yesterday that her passing to and fro disturbed me. Today, I heard that tonga of hers coming in this direction. I was swimming in the lake. I waited until she was near enough to get a clear view, and then I surreptitiously removed my bathing trunks and emerged—a splendid figure of nude manhood —and proceeded to do my usual exercises."

"You"—Cosmo stopped and drew a long breath—"you . . . did you say you . . ."

"As naked as the day I was born. I hope she found pleasure in the sight—but I shall never know. The pony, which had been ambling along at its usual pace, suddenly broke into a gallop, and the cart, with Lady Laura, went out of sight. She won't be round this way again."

There was a long silence. Hallam, swinging, waited for his guest to recover. "Something's happened, hasn't it?" he asked at last. "Today, I mean."

Cosmo, with a great effort, brought his mind back to his own affairs. "No." He remembered the letter, and grew pale. "Well, yes, in a way."

"Lady Laura bit you?"

"Oh no, no, no. I haven't seen her today. It's just that . . . well, I went to my office and there was a . . . a letter."

"And the letter upset you?"

"Yes, it did, rather."

"Are its contents a secret?"

Cosmo hesitated. "No. The letter . . . yes, I suppose in a way. But on the other hand . . ."

Hallam wondered if he had made the drinks too strong. He had intended to throw a beneficent haze over the old man's troubles, but he seemed to have overdone it. Or perhaps not—talking to him at any time required skill and patience.

"Who wrote the letter?" he asked.

Cosmo did not answer for some time. When he did, his tone was absent, almost dreamy. "You don't know much about this place, do you?" he asked. "The Manor, I mean. You've never——"

"——been interested? Yes and no. When I decided to come here, I tried to find out something about its history. What I found was that there didn't seem to be any history worth recording."

"May I ask," Cosmo ventured timidly, "why you came here? It doesn't seem a place . . . I mean to say, there must be many other places where . . ."

"I came because I wanted a kind of hideout. A retreat. I had to get away somewhere, to some place where I could work without interruptions. You see, some years ago, I wrote a book on the approach to archaeology. I wrote it for my three young brothers, in the hope of getting them interested in the subject. They took the typescript with them to read at school, and the headmaster saw it, read it and arranged to have it published. It caught on, and now it's a school textbook and the publishers want it revised. I started on the revision in London, found I had too many friends, looked for a place to which they wouldn't want to follow me and found this."

"And you can work here?"

"Look for yourself. Beauty, seclusion and—now that I've

got rid of the tonga and its occupant—peace. Added to which, Rivering's a dull town, too dull to attract my friends; the house I'm renting from Lady Laura is too small to fit guests, the hotel is or was closed, and the other place—the pub, the inn, the White Hart—doesn't provide civilized amenities. But what really made me decide to come here was this summerhouse. When I came down to look at the house . . ."

"How did you hear of it?"

"I caught a glimpse of the summerhouse, and told Lady Laura I'd like to rent it. She agreed, so I decided I'd use the house for my luggage and spend my days here by the lake. I knew I wouldn't be bothered by outsiders—Lady Laura told me that the public was allowed into the grounds only on certain days, and when they enter, they pay. How did I hear of the house? From a journalist friend who came down to include the Manor in his series on *son et lumière*. And now we can revert to the fatal letter you received this morning."

"Fatal? Hardly that," Cosmo said. "You wouldn't be able to understand why the letter worried me because, as you said just now, you know nothing of the history of the Manor. Certainly it is not an exciting history, but—"

"You can relate as much or as little of it as I have to know before being told what was in that letter. Begin. No, don't. Let me refill these glasses first." He refilled them and climbed back into the hammock. "Ready, go."

"My father," Cosmo began, "wrote a short history of Stapling Manor. I think he hoped to publish it, but he died soon after writing it. The manuscript was among his papers, and I thought then, and still think, that I should have sent it to a publisher and—"

Off the point again, Hallam thought irritably. Question and answer was the only way. "Were you born in Rivering?" he asked.

"Yes, I was." Cosmo stared into his glass. "It all seems a very long time ago. I used to be sent for to play with Lady Helen—she and I were not the same age, but—"

"Why did you have to be sent for? Didn't you like girls?"

"She was away at school a good deal of the time. During the holidays, there weren't many young people . . . I mean to say that in those days, though this may sound archaic to you, she wasn't allowed to—"

"—associate with all and sundry. Who exactly was this overprotected Lady Helen?"

"She was the earl's daughter—his only child. The earl of Bosfield. The last earl of Bosfield."

"And he was brother to Lady Laura?"

"Yes."

"That makes Lady Laura the aunt of Lady Helen. Proceed."

"She was a very pretty little girl—Lady Helen, I mean. They were a good-looking family."

"Judging by Lady Laura, I'd say they were. How old is she?"

"Lady Laura?" Cosmo considered. "She was born . . . let me see . . . she's seventy-two."

"How long has she owned this place?"

"Owned?" Cosmo gave a brief, hopeless sigh. "That's just the trouble. She doesn't own this place."

Hallam hitched himself up in the hammock and for the first time displayed real interest. "So that's it," he said slowly. "I suppose you think I'm a fool for not having asked you before."

"Once, I would have told you. Once, when she entered into negotiations with people, I used to think it my duty to explain that she was not in a position to enter into—"

"That's why there was no written contract, I suppose, when she leased the house and the summerhouse?"

"That is why. You would have found out that she was not

the owner if you had spent more time down in the town. Everybody in Rivering knows the truth, but—like me—they've come to accept the situation. Did you ask for a written contract?"

"No. She said that she didn't like lawyers and all she would ever consent to was what she called a gentlemen's agreement. She said the Moultons, and yourself, had had a gentlemen's agreement with her for over twenty-five years. I suppose the Moultons know she isn't the owner?"

"Yes. They've always known. As I said, everybody knows. That's one reason I have so few clients—people won't come to me because they know I made a hash of my duties as trustee. They won't—"

"Trustee of what? Trustee for whom?" Hallam leaned back. "Look, let's begin at the beginning," he suggested. "Not the entire history—we can skip that. As I said, I dug into it before coming here, and came up with nothing. All I've gleaned since coming here was when the *son et lumière* season opened and I walked over and sat on one of those hard benches and . . ."

"That," Cosmo said, "wasn't real history."

Hallam frowned. "I bought a booklet. It was there, all neatly printed. I read it as I sat on the hard bench waiting for the show to begin. It was a good show."

"But pure invention."

"Invention? You mean none of those episodes ever took place?"

"None. It was all fictitious."

"But damn it, that's cheating!" Hallam protested. "It's deluding the public. Who invented it—your father?"

"No, no, no! Most certainly not. No. My father did years of research when he was writing the history. His was all quite authentic. He went up to London and examined various documents, he went to the British Museum, he . . ."

"Did he ever show it to Lady Laura?"

"Yes."

"Then why did she have to invent? Why didn't she use authentic bits for her *son et lumière*?"

"Because, as you yourself observed, it was not an exciting history. There were no exciting episodes, in fact, the family history is one of studious, of deliberate avoidance of excitement. If you had been at all interested, I could have told you . . ."

"I wasn't. Now I am. Go back to the beginning."

"My father couldn't trace much before 1490. That was the year the Manor was built."

"Why did he want to go back further than that?"

"Because it was built on the site of a previous Manor, which had been destroyed by Sir Richard Stapling's enemies. Do you know—that is to say—do you remember anything about the Wars of the Roses?"

"I suppose so. Let me see . . . Yorkists versus Lancastrians. Half a minute and I'll tell you who won. The Yorkists did. The poor old Lancastrians got it in the neck more than once —Mortimer's Cross, February the second, 1461. My God, fancy my being able to disinter that fact after fifteen or more years. I can disinter some more, I think. Hedgeley Moor and Hexham—both, if I'm right, in 1464. Who was it who wrote: 'For old, forgotten, far-off things/And battles long ago'?"

"It was Wordsworth. But it wasn't 'forgotten, far-off things.' He wrote 'unhappy, far-off things.' "

"He should have written 'forgotten.' More alliterative. Which battles were we talking about?"

"You had got to Hexham."

"Then there was Tewkesbury. I've forgotten the date, but wasn't it at Tewkesbury that the young Prince Edward was killed and Queen Margaret—was it Margaret?—captured?

"Yes."

"I must have been a brighter boy at school than anybody suspected. What happened after that? Oh, yes—Henry VI was killed, and the House of York firmly established on the English throne. Game, set and match to the Yorkists."

"No."

"No?"

"There was one representative of the Lancastrians left."

"So there was. Henry Tudor, earl of Richmond. But he was in exile."

"He came back from exile in 1485. The king, Richard the Third, was—"

"—defeated and killed at the Battle of Bosworth. After which, Henry Tudor was proclaimed king, and by his marriage to I forget whom, united the houses of York and Lancaster and they all lived happily ever after. So what does all that have to do with Stapling Manor?"

"Everything. Sir Richard Stapling was a knight in the service of Henry Tudor. While he was in exile with his master, the Manor of Stapling was attacked by his enemies, and destroyed—levelled. When Henry Tudor was proclaimed king after the Battle of Bosworth, he dubbed Sir Richard Stapling earl of Bosfield. The earl returned to Stapling and rebuilt the Manor on the site of the one that had been destroyed and from that time onward, the tradition of the family was to avoid conflicts. The Manor was built as strongly as it was possible to build—granite, moat, surrounding wall. Within the wall, successive earls were born, and died, but not one took part in any contemporary struggle if he could avoid it. They had, after Bosworth, no history whatsoever. Mention any great battle; you will find that there was—"

"—no Stapling present. But they must have changed the tradition. Didn't the last earl die in the first World War?"

"Yes, he did but oddly enough, not in battle. He died as the result of a kick from his horse. That was in 1914. He married just before being sent over to France. His daughter was born in 1915, and lived at the Manor with her mother."

"And this daughter was Lady Helen?"

"Yes."

"Where was Lady Laura?"

"She lived at the Manor too, with her brother's widow. They didn't get on well together. When her sister-in-law died, Lady Laura went on living there with Lady Helen—not happily."

"They didn't get on either?"

"It's not too much, I think," Cosmo said slowly, "to say that Lady Helen hated her. Then war broke out—the second World War. In 1943, some Americans were sent to Rivering, and Lady Helen fell in love with one of them. Lady Laura did all she could to prevent them from marrying, but the marriage took place, and Lady Helen went to live in America. Lady Laura moved almost at once into the solar wing, and it's as well she did, because shortly afterwards, two bombs fell on the grounds. One left the central part of the Manor the shell you see now. The other destroyed part of the wall and made an enormous crater into which the water from the moat began to flow."

"Crater? You mean this lake?"

"Yes. There was no lake before. The Americans did wonders. They shored up the banks of the crater, they let the lake fill—at Lady Laura's request—and they separated it from the moat. They also collected all the scattered granite and put it near the gap in the wall so that Lady Laura could—"

"You mean she actually built those three houses—yours and mine and the Moultons'—in the gap?"

"Yes."

"Was that one of the things you tried to stop her from doing?"

"Yes."

"Because she wasn't the owner?"

"She had no right to do any of the things she . . ."

"The owner, I presume, is the Lady Helen we've been talking about?"

"She was. She died six years after her marriage, leaving a daughter of three."

"And this daughter, now aged three plus, is the present owner?"

"Yes. She lives in America."

"Have you kept in touch?"

"No. The last communication I had with her father was just after his wife, Lady Helen, died. He wrote to tell me that he had decided to say nothing about her inheritance to his daughter until she grew up and was of an age to—"

"—take it in. And when she grew up, and he told her, what did . . ."

"He never told her. The first she knew about the Manor, and her ownership of it, was after her father's death, which took place a year ago. He had kept all the papers and the letters, and she read them."

"And then?"

"She decided to come to England."

"It can't have taken her a year to get to England."

"She left America about two months ago. She wrote to me from Paris. She didn't say exactly when she would be coming to Stapling, but—"

"—but she's coming. How old is she?"

"Twenty-three."

"And you're upset—here we come to the core at last—you're upset because you're afraid she'll arrive, size up the situation and then proceed to turn out all the tenants—which include yourself and myself—and denounce the *son et lumière* as a fraud, and sue her great-aunt, Lady Laura, for damages. That's it, isn't it?"

"Oh, no, no, no! Don't you see? I was her trustee. Her affairs were in my hands. I've betrayed my trust."

"But you haven't pocketed any of the profits—why should you get into a state of panic?"

"I have a strong sense of duty but I have not been strong

(45)

enough to carry out this duty. The earl appointed first my father, then myself, trustee. I shall have to account to the owner. I shall have to take her round the estate. She will see everything that Lady Laura has done. She will come expecting nothing but a ruin—she will have read my letter written after the bombs fell, and she will look for a ruin, and what will she find? The solar wing of the Manor beautifully restored, and Lady Laura in residence. Flowers grown for sale. Three houses built with their backs joined to the wall of the Manor. The public admitted to the grounds. The summerhouse let. The stables let. Performances of *son et lumière*. Don't you see the position I'm in? What sort of man shall I appear? What shall I say? What shall I do?"

"Point out how fortunate she is. Instead of a ruin, she'll see a flourishing estate. Her property has been used, rebuilt, transformed."

"Without reference to, without permission from herself. And for motives of profit, profit that has gone—"

"—into Lady Laura's pocket. What did she live on before she began robbing the owner?"

"She never had any money. The family fortunes have steadily declined. There was a great deal to begin with—enormous grants of land and money—but today there is virtually nothing. The last saleable acre has been sold. Rents ceased to come in many years ago. What money there was, was traditionally used to keep the Manor in repair—that is why it stood for so long. All Lady Laura had was the money her niece, Lady Helen, turned over to her when she left the Manor—it was the residue of the Stapling capital. It was not a large sum. Lady Helen's husband offered a generous settlement, but Lady Laura would accept nothing from him."

"Who was he?"

"His name was Berg. He owned a ranch in Arizona and was said to be a millionaire."

"And that was the match you said Lady Laura opposed?"

"Yes. She didn't like him. He seemed to me an excellent young man; there was no reason for her dislike, none whatever. But she treated him in rather a high-handed way, and it proved the last straw for Lady Helen. She left the Manor saying that she would never return to it while her aunt was alive. And I should have sent her regular reports about what was going on here, but I didn't, because I found myself quite helpless at managing Lady Laura. I hoped, I believed I would be dead before being called to account—and now I have this letter in my pocket telling me that the owner is coming."

"Keep it in your pocket," Hallam advised.

"Keep it . . . but I must tell Lady Laura about it, and—"

"Why must you? This girl, this Berg, left America over two months ago and hasn't got here yet. That doesn't indicate any excessive interest in her inheritance, does it?"

"No, but—"

"If she'd really wanted to see it, she wouldn't have detoured for two months. She probably won't turn up at all. If she does, what will there be here to interest her? The money Lady Laura has been and is pocketing will look like loose change to a millionaire's daughter. There's nowhere for her to stay—Lady Laura certainly won't invite her to share the solar wing. The hotel, I'm told, isn't open, and the White Hart's not for young women from the land of good plumbing. If she comes, which I doubt, all you have to do is point to the improvements. She'll have herself photographed with Lady Laura against the historic background, and go home to her ranch. Now stop worrying."

"But Lady Laura—"

"Lady Laura," Hallam said, rolling out of the hammock and picking up the empty glasses, "expected to be left here, undisturbed, for the rest of her life. So she proceeded to make hay, and I don't blame her. Forget the whole thing. I'm going to fetch that cheese, and the pâté, and we're going to sit out here and eat." He refilled the glasses and handed one to Cosmo. "The next time you come, bring your father's brief history; I'd like to read it. Do you like your tomatoes whole, or sliced and dressed?"

"Oh, whole, thank you."

"Then let's eat. But first we drink." He raised his glass. "To the rightful owner," he toasted. "Long may she stay away."

CHAPTER

3

On a wet evening at the end of June, Nell and Mrs. Saltry drove into Rivering in a hired car and stopped at the entrance to the White Hart. Nell switched off the engine and for a time the two sat in silence, gazing at the scene before them.

The town could seldom have looked less inviting. It was the end of a market day; rain was still pouring down, forming miniature lakes on the sodden, sagging canvas shelters erected over the market stalls, and spilling in a steady stream onto the puddles below. Some of the stalls were already closed; at others, figures in dripping mackintoshes were packing unsold produce into boxes and crates and loading them onto waiting vans. The last buyers were splashing their way between the lines of stalls, treading underfoot vegetables which had fallen and been left lying among the litter. The shops round the square were shuttered, the offices empty. The windows of the café were misted and an unseen, doubtless juvenile artist was drawing rudimentary designs on the panes. From the overcrowded entrance lounge of the White Hart issued a loud buzz of conversation.

"Merrie England," Mrs. Saltry said bitterly. Her eyes went from the shabby inn, with its faded and discoloured sign, its uncompromising and unwelcoming front, to the newly-painted, recently-reopened hotel on the other side of the square. "Even if we could have got rooms at that place, I wouldn't have liked it any better than this dump."

Nell laughed. "There's no use in sitting here," she said. "I'll go inside and find someone to get the stuff out of the car."

"I'll come with you. Maybe it'll be warmer in there. Can I borrow your coat, Nell, if you're not using it?"

"Sure. Here—take it."

Mrs. Saltry put it on and they went together into the noisy, steaming mouth of the inn. There was scarcely a woman in sight. Burly farmers in damp mackintoshes and gaiters stood talking in groups; those who made way for the newcomers did so with a grudging air.

Arriving at last at the reception desk, Nell and Mrs. Saltry found nobody in attendance. After waiting for some time, Nell knocked loudly on the counter. From behind the small switchboard came a low moan.

"Go away, whoever you are," begged an afflicted voice. "Just go away."

From a doorway behind the switchboard appeared a long-haired, bewhiskered youth wearing jeans and a pink satin shirt. He surveyed the visitors through small, uninterested eyes.

"Evenin'," he said laconically. "If it's dinner you're after, you'll have a long wait. First lot's going in now, and the tables is all booked for the second go. If you'd like to sit in the bar, it's through there." He jerked a thumb and turned away, his duty done, to address the invisible moaner. "Oh, come on, Betsy. Perk up, why don't you?"

Betsy—portly, middle-aged and haggard—came into sight

and sank on to a chair behind the counter. She closed her eyes, clutched her head and gave a loud groan.

"If you go drinking with the customers, you know what to expect," the youth told her severely. "I've told you and told you—you can't hold it, so why take it? A couple of beers, and look what they do to you. Week after week, you go'n dish yourself. Every market day, you . . ."

"Oh shut up, Charley, do." A girl, tall and thin, had come from the direction of the bar. "Leave Betsy alone. Give her an aspirin or something. And ask those two people what they want and tell them we're not taking no more orders for dinner."

"I told them they'd have to wait," Charley answered.

Mrs. Saltry spoke in a crisp voice. "Will you please have our luggage brought out of the car?" she requested.

There was a pause. The girl and Charley stared. Even Betsy opened her eyes for a few moments.

"Americans," Charley announced at last to the thin girl. "We don't get many 'ere, do we, Daise?"

"Not all that many," Daise agreed. "And mostly coach trips."

"Will you show us to our rooms, please?" Mrs. Saltry demanded.

"*Rooms?*" echoed Charley in astonishment.

"What rooms?" Daise asked.

"The rooms we reserved. My name is Mrs. Saltry. I have reservations—one room with a bath and one room without a bath because there wasn't a bath."

"You mean you *booked?*" Charley asked, still amazed.

"That's right. I booked."

"Well, I don't know nothing about that," he said doubtfully. "I'm not in charge, see? I'm only supposed to help in the bar. Know anything about bookings, Daise?"

"Not a thing."

"When was it you booked for?" Charley inquired.

"For today," Mrs. Saltry told him. "I reserved the rooms

more than a week ago. You confirmed the reservation with the agents in London."

"Agents? I never heard of no agents," Charley said in a dazed voice. "You know anything about agents, Daise?"

"No. How should I know anything about agents?" Daise asked indignantly.

"Here, Betsy." Charley turned to appeal to the sufferer. "You know anything about bookings and agents?"

"Oh, use your head," groaned Betsy. "Get Mike—he's the one who does bookings. And get me those aspirins while you're about it."

"Yes, get Mike," Daise advised.

"If I want to get Mike," Charley said, "I'll 'ave to go all the way to Stratford, because that's where he is."

"Mike—at Stratford? What's he doing at Stratford?" Daise asked with interest.

"I wouldn't like to say," Charley answered.

"What—you don't mean he's gone after that girl, do you?" Daise asked. "Did he tell you her name?"

"No, he didn't. When I asked him, he said she was called Anne Hathaway. I was going to laugh, but he said it real nasty, so I didn't."

"But it's not his day off," Daise pointed out. "What's he doing going off to Stratford when it isn't his day off?"

"Oh, stop jawing and get me some aspirins, will you?" Betsy said on a high note. "I'm suffering—can't you see?"

"Half a mo'," Charley said. "Got to fix up the customers first."

"If they booked," Daise said impatiently, "it'll have to be in the book, won't it?"

"Only if Mike put it there," Charley answered.

"Well, you can look, can't you, fathead?" Daise came forward, seized a large black book and began to turn its pages irritably. "I wish you'd show some gumption sometimes, Charley, really I do. Yes, here it is. Number five and number seven. Number five and number seven empty, Betsy?"

"Suppose so. How do I know? Charley, will you get those aspirins before I pass out?"

"I'll get them," Daise said. "Charley, you take the customers up to number five and number seven. If there's someone else in them, that's not my fault."

"The luggage," Mrs. Saltry told Charley, "is out in the car."

"Right-o." He pushed his way through the crowd and then reappeared. "Which car?" he asked.

"The blue one at the door," Nell told him.

He left them, but not for long. "No car outside the door," he reported, "blue or pink." He looked at Daise, who had brought a packet of aspirins and was shaking out two for Betsy. "What'll you bet it's that Ernie Lauder again?" he asked her. "Getting to be a disease with him. Hardly waits for the passengers to get out before he nips it away."

"Well, you can't blame him," Daise pointed out reasonably. "I mean to say, if people left cars all over the square on a market day, where'd we be? Ernie's right to tow them away."

Mrs. Saltry stared at her in horror. "Tow? You don't mean—"

"Didn't you see a policeman out there when you came?" Charley asked her. "You must have—try'n think. Tall chap with a nasty expression. He's always on duty on market days, and he nips cars away quick as a flash. If you'd told me when you first came in here that you'd left a car outside, I'd have warned you. But you didn't say nothing about a car, only about bookings and agents; that's the way we wasted a lot of time, see?"

"Where have they taken the car to?" Nell asked him.

"They tow 'em over to Wedderly."

"And where's Wedderly?"

(53)

"About four miles. There's a short cut if you want to walk, but this isn't weather for walking, is it?"

"Would you call a cab, please?" Mrs. Saltry requested.

"A—? Oh, a taxi. It's no use calling, not on market day," Charley answered. "They're all busy. If you go outside and wait, I daresay one'll turn up. You'd do better to wait till morning—plenty of taxis to be had tomorrow."

"I'd like my luggage tonight, thank you. Come on, Nell."

"Why don't you wait here?" Nell suggested. "I'll go and get the car."

Mrs. Saltry gave a glance round the lounge, and shuddered. "I'm going with you," she said.

Charlie lent them a large umbrella, and they went to the entrance and peered out through the rain. The square had almost emptied; the last vans were moving away under the eye of a tall policeman whose helmet and thick mackintosh made him indifferent to the downpour. Mrs. Saltry eyed him balefully.

"Ernie Lauder. Look at him, smug as they come. Nothing to do but stand there and tow cars away, and not even offering to call a cab. I'm going over and . . ."

"No, you're not. You're staying here."

"Why shouldn't I tell him what I—"

"No. We're in enough trouble," Nell said firmly. "You stay right here beside this door, and I'll get a cab."

A taxi came in sight, and she darted forward, but before she could raise a hand to attract the driver's attention, two women had emerged from behind the market stalls, hailed him and driven away. The next taxi to appear was taken by a couple with three children. Nell was ready for the next one; she stopped it in mid-square, climbed in and directed the driver to the inn to pick up Mrs. Saltry. Then they drove along a straight, uninteresting road lined at intervals by small, whitewashed cottages. Wedderly was merely a cluster of larger houses built round a village pond; it might have been called picturesque if the huge, barn-like structure a short distance away could have been removed. The taxi driver jerked a thumb towards it.

"You'll find your car in there," he said. "Want me to wait in case there's a hitch?"

"No, thank you." Mrs. Saltry's manner indicated that she was prepared to deal with hitches. "Come on, Nell."

Inside the building were about a dozen cars lined up in military formation. A stout policeman seated at a desk beckoned Nell and Mrs. Saltry forward, asked their names and then gave them a fatherly talk about the advisability of parking in official parking lots.

"If that young constable hadn't been on duty," he ended, "you might have got away with it, but he's very particular about parked cars. If your car had had an American license plate, he'd have put a warning slip inside. It's a pity to have to pay a fine, but I'm afraid I'll have to ask you to."

They paid it, got into the car and drove away.

"When we get back to that inn," Mrs. Saltry said, "I'm not getting out until you've found out where their garage is, if they've got a garage. If they tow the car away while you're asking, they'll have to tow me, too. You know something, Nell? If I don't get a drink soon, I'll die, really die."

"I'll see you get one, as soon as we've gotten rid of the car."

Getting rid of the car meant driving round to the garage behind the inn and waiting until Charley had cleared a way between two large vans. Back at the inn, Mrs. Saltry spoke firmly.

"The luggage can go up," she said, "but I'm going to find that bar. If the rooms upstairs are anything like the rooms downstairs, I'll need a drink before I see them."

They walked across the lounge, which during their absence had become depopulated, but Mrs. Saltry's observation that the farmers had gone home was proved incorrect when they passed the dining room and saw burly figures occupying every table. On opening the door leading to the bar, they were met by a powerful smell of beer and a roar of conversation from a throng so tightly packed that fighting their way through it to order drinks would have been almost impossible. Mrs. Saltry closed the door again and marched to the reception desk. Charley came in answer to her imperious knocking on the counter, and gazed at her in surprise.

"Thought you'd gone to have a drink," he said.

"We can't get into the bar. Will you please take us up to our rooms?"

He studied her tight lips and angry, gleaming eyes and then lifted the flap of the counter, came out and led the way to the stairs, addressing them over his shoulder as he went.

"I'll tell you how it is. Other days, we're just a nice, quiet, cosy pub with a few customers we can attend to—but market days, that's something else. I thought that now the hotel was opened, we'd lose half our customers, but they didn't know it was open, so we got the lot. Tomorrow, you'll get all the service you want, quick and willing. Here y'are. Number five. That's the one without the bath, so I suppose it'll be for the young lady. Yes? In you go, Miss. And here's number seven. Smells a bit musty, but don't let that put you off; the bed's nice and comfy and there's all the hot water you need. I wouldn't open the window if I was you, not in weather like this. The wind brings the rain in." He withdrew to the thinly-carpeted corridor. "Anything else I can do for you?"

He was gone before Mrs. Saltry could decide whether a tip was or was not in order.

"No, no tip," said Nell. "When we go away. Do you want me to open your window?"

"You don't think I could sleep in this atmosphere, do you?" Mrs. Saltry demanded.

Nell, after a brief struggle, got the window open. A blast of cold wind brought in, as Charley had foretold, a spatter of rain.

"Can't you nearly close it and just leave a little air I can breathe?" Mrs. Saltry wailed.

Nell, after experimenting, shook her head. "Open or shut," she stated. "It hasn't got anything in between."

Mrs. Saltry moaned. "Come here and feel this bed, Nell. Lumps. Did you ever see a bed this size before? It isn't double, it's treble. And that isn't a bathroom at all—it's just a bit they've partitioned off, and they haven't even bothered to hide the pipes. How long, for God's sake, do we have to stay here?"

"Maybe they'll have some rooms over at the hotel—cancellations or something."

"Not a chance. The agent told me they were booked for weeks ahead, with a waiting list. Would you believe that so many people would want to come to this town? Well, we're stuck in it for just as long as it takes you to inspect your ruin and your great-aunt. And I don't want to put on any pressure, but I don't think I can take much of this."

"You're hungry, like me," Nell diagnosed. "Let's go down and eat."

Halfway down, they met Charley coming up. "Just going to fetch you," he said. "Got a table, but you'd better get in there quick. They want to get finished and cleared away."

The dining room was now half empty, but none of the vacant tables had been cleared. There was only one waitress in attendance—a short, sturdy girl so intent on her duties that she had the expression of a sleepwalker. As Nell and Mrs. Saltry entered, she swept past them, balancing three plates laden with food; jerking her hand in the direction of a littered table, she spoke mechanically.

"Over there. Shan't be long."

They took their places, and Nell pushed the dirty plates to one side. They sat for some time in silence, Mrs. Saltry's eyes following the bee-like flight of the waitress. "We'll sit here till Thanksgiving Day," she said at last. "The more I sit, the less hungry I get. How about you?"

Nell made no reply. She was noting what the more fortunate customers were eating, and was rapidly reaching the point at which she felt she would snatch the food on its way to their mouths.

The waitress came at last, swept the debris from the table onto the adjacent one, and without ceremony laid two steaming plates of food before them.

"Sorry, no choice," she intoned. "Take it or leave it, apple tart to follow, beer or mineral water."

"No beer, thank you," said Mrs. Saltry. "I'd like a . . ."

"Two beers," interposed Nell. "It's no use," she continued, when the waitress had darted away. "You won't get anything fancy. She's too busy, for one thing—and for another, they wouldn't have it in a place like this. The food"—she spoke through a mouthful—"is marvellous. Go ahead and eat."

"I couldn't, Nell. All I want is—"

"I know. But you won't get it, so it's no use asking. This is a place for farmers, and thank goodness, farmers know how to eat. It may not be what's written on the diet charts, but it's great, just great. If you can't finish all of yours, I'll have some of it."

Mrs. Saltry transhipped a large wedge of pastry, a piece of steak, two kidneys, three potatoes and a mountain of cabbage. Nell got through it with as much dispatch as she could, for Mrs. Saltry, after the first mouthful, showed signs of wanting some of it back again.

"If you asked me, Corinne," she said at last, mopping up the last gleam of gravy with a piece of bread and wiping her mouth on the small square of paper napkin, "if you asked me which I'd go for, a fancy dining room with tidbits, or spots on the cloth and marvellous food like this, I know which I'd choose. Are you going to eat all that apple tart?"

"Yes, I am."

"It's kind of fattening, isn't it?"

"It's nourishing, and at this moment I need nourishment."

"Would there be second helpings, do you suppose?"

They asked the waitress, who said there were no second helpings. The woman at the next table, overhearing, leaned over and seized her companion's plate just as he was about to embark on his portion.

"Here, you eat my husband's," she said, holding out the plate to Nell. "He doesn't want it."

Her husband, barrel-shaped, red-faced and with an overstuffed look, spoke gruffly. "He do want it. But he won't get it."

"That's right, he won't," confirmed his wife, and turned to Nell. "Go on, deary, you eat it up and enjoy it. If he gets through any more, he'll burst. I'm not saying he's greedy; he just doesn't know when to stop. Americans, aren't you? We don't get many round here. They come in coaches twice a week for the show up at the Manor, and then they go away again. They used to eat here, but from now on, they'll go and eat at that hotel across the square. It's a shame, taking good business away from this place."

"Aye. The old witch," growled her husband vindictively.

His wife pushed the bill towards him.

"Hold your tongue and pay that," she ordered. "You needn't leave any extra—it's all in."

They rose, said goodbye and added their good wishes for a nice holiday. Then they went away, leaving Nell staring after them uneasily. "Who did he call an old witch?" she asked. "And what's the show up at the Manor?"

"How do I know? You can find that out from the lawyer tomorrow. What time are you going to his office?"

"About ten o'clock, I guess. He'd be there by then, wouldn't he?"

"I can't understand why he didn't answer your letter. Why don't you call him in the morning?"

"He couldn't answer my letter. I told him I was moving around. You're coming with me to see him, aren't you?"

"I'll go with you, but I'm not going to sit in while you're talking to him. That's your business. I'll stay in the waiting room—there'll be some kind of waiting room—until you're through." She stopped and sneezed. "Nell, I've got to get into some warmer clothes. This cold is going right through my bones."

They stopped at the counter on their way to their rooms. Nell's intention had been to put a few questions about the Manor to Charley, but a piece of paper propped on the counter bore the words: *Staff at Supper,* and only Betsy, one hand holding a damp handkerchief to her head, was on duty. They walked across the lounge, opened the door of a room marked *Residents Only,* found it filled with non-residents singing loudly, and went slowly up to their rooms.

"I'm going to get right into bed and try to get warm," Mrs. Saltry announced. "How about you?"

"I'll read, maybe."

"If you want to use my bathroom, you're welcome."

"No, thank you. I'm not far away from the one at the end of the corridor. I'd like to get up early and kind of look around before we go to the lawyer's. Want to come?"

"No. I want my coffee at half past eight—up here. Do you suppose they've ever served breakfast to anyone in their room?"

"I'll make them. Good night."

"A good night," Mrs. Saltry prophesied, "it will *not* be."

Nell was awake at half past seven, and out of the inn by eight. She had to pass through a ghostly, still-darkened lounge, in which no effort had yet been made at clearing last night's disorder. The telephone switchboard was unattended. The large double doors of the entrance were closed but not locked, and she opened them and stepped out into the bright morning with a sigh of relief and pleasure.

The market square was empty, the shops still closed. A milk float went clanking on its rounds; a boy on a bicycle delivered newspapers. She walked towards the river—almost every road in Rivering, she found after a time, led to the river. She walked slowly, reflecting that her mother must have walked past these houses, must have known the market square and the inn, perhaps had come to this quiet path along the river's edge.

Driving into Rivering the evening before, she had seen, beside a road which led uphill, a sign which had read: *No Through Road. Stapling Manor Only.* Soon she would drive up the road, up the hill, and she would see it. Stapling Manor.

But however long its history, it had come to an end. Nearly five hundred years of Staplings, father to son—but somewhere in Sweden, there must be Bergs who went back as far as the Staplings—only they hadn't been earls and they hadn't kept records, and so her ancestry had this lop-sided look, so much on one side, so little on the other. She was a Berg; she should have been standing now in a town in Sweden, tracing her past, but nobody had ever been able to discover exactly which town great-grandfather Berg had left in order to settle in America. All that was known was that he had brought nothing with him—nothing but his capacity for hard work, and his creed, passed down to his American descendants, to save one dollar for every three dollars earned.

She walked slowly back to the inn. The doors were open, and last night's waitress was wielding a vacuum cleaner with the same speed and concentration she had shown with plates. As there was still no sign of life at the reception counter, Nell attempted to ask, over the whirring of the cleaner, for some breakfast, but the ex-waitress merely gazed at her unseeingly and sent the machine in a wide arc round the displaced chairs and tables.

Nell glanced at the clock—nearly nine. She walked round pressing every bell in sight; nobody answered the summons. The cleaner whirred without ceasing.

Anger, slow to rise, filled her. She marched in the direction of the dining room, went through it without pausing, and entered a vast kitchen. At its far end she saw Charley seated at a table eating bacon and eggs, a newspaper propped against the coffeepot.

"Good morning." She halted before him. "I hope I'm not disturbing your breakfast."

He looked up at her. He had not been over-bright the evening before; this morning he looked limp and vapid.

"Eh?"

"Did you get your own breakfast, or did someone bring it to you?"

"This?"

"Yes. The bacon and the eggs and the coffee."

"I did it myself, of course," he said in surprise. "You don't think they wait on me here, do you?"

"They certainly don't wait on guests. Who's supposed to get breakfast for Mrs. Saltry, and for me?"

"Not my job," he said resentfully, through a mouthful of egg. "You have to ring your bell and ask."

"I rang every bell there was. Nobody came. The only people alive in the building, besides myself and Mrs. Saltry are the waitress, who's cleaning, and yourself, eating. If you'll please tell me where the things are kept, I'll get my own breakfast."

"You can't do that!" he protested.

"No? Watch me."

Banging cupboard doors, diving into recesses, she assembled frying pan, coffeepot, coffee, milk, sugar, eggs and the last two slices of bacon. She put the coffeepot on the stove, found two trays and saw with satisfaction that her actions were making Charley too uneasy to allow him to continue eating.

"Hey, look, you're going to get me into trouble—or yourself into trouble," he told her. "You can't come in here and make yourself at home, you know. This kitchen is for the staff."

"Don't you talk to me," she snapped. "I'm busy, can't you see? When I go back to America, I'm going to write an article for the newspapers on English inns, naming this one as the worst. See if I don't. I wish I could include a picture of you sitting there taking it easy while the guests do the work. No, don't get up. Just go on reading your paper. I don't want you to cook my eggs, thank you—I don't want them floating in nasty grease like yours are, with leathery bottoms. And I don't like the look of that coffee, either. If you sent any of that up to Mrs. Saltry, she'd send it straight back again."

He had left the rest of his breakfast and was making attempts to assist her. She swept him aside.

"You keep away," she warned. "I'm doing all right."

"Here's Betsy," he said with relief. "Look what she's doing, Betsy. I told her to ring her bell and wait, but she wouldn't."

"I like my breakfast at breakfast time," Nell informed them. "Mrs. Saltry likes hers up in her room and that's where she's going to have it."

"No meals in rooms," Betsy said firmly. "Dining room only."

"I'm not going to wait until those dirty cloths are taken off the tables," said Nell. "Watch." She broke an egg neatly and dropped it into the frying pan, where it nestled against the bacon. "I'm going to eat in here and then I'm going to take my coffee upstairs and have it with Mrs. Saltry. And if you won't do it tomorrow morning, I'll go to the mayor or the sheriff, or both, and make a complaint. Pass over those rolls, please."

She seated herself at a corner of the long trestle table and began to eat. Charley and Betsy watched her morosely.

"I suppose you think," Betsy said resentfully, "that we can be on our feet till after two in the morning, and then go dancing up the stairs with coffee at dawn? Do you know how many people it'd take to staff this place, if we could get the staff to staff this place? We'd need four if not six more of us."

Nell looked up. "Who's in charge?" she inquired.

"I am. My dad's the owner, but he's never here. Time and time again I've said to him: 'Dad,' I've said, 'the only thing that keeps this place going is the food and drink, so why bother with rooms? It doesn't pay, and it makes too much work. Why not just a pub,' I keeping saying, 'with plates of good food at the bar?' But does he listen? No." She took the coffeepot off the stove and brought it to Nell. "Couldn't spare a cup, could you?"

"Help yourself," Nell said. "And tell Charley to make some more for Mrs. Saltry, the way I made it, and take it up to her."

"Take it *up* to her?" Charley repeated in a high, horrified tone. "Take it *up* to her? Me?"

"Yes, you," Nell said.

"What—me, a man—go into 'er room first thing in the morning, someone of 'er age, before ever she's out of bed, and I don't even know 'er? What d'you take me for?"

"A member of the staff doing waiter's duties," Nell told him. "The morning tea in every big hotel is brought in by waiters, and as far as I know, they've all survived."

"Well, I'm not going to do it, and that's flat."

"Then you can carry up the tray when it's ready, and I'll take it at the door."

"That much," he conceded, "I'll do, but you won't get me to act bedroom waiter."

He put more coffee on the stove and then came to lean against the table and look at Nell.

"Look, what brings you to Rivering?" he asked. "I know it's not my business, but I'd like to know. There's nothing 'ere for anybody like you. D'you know anybody 'ere, like?"

"I came to see Stapling Manor."

"But what's to see in Stapling Manor?" he asked.

"It's a historic ruin, isn't it?"

"Not the sort people come to see—not people from a long way off, like you, not unless it's on the nights they have that sonny loom. It isn't what you'd call a famous place, is it, Betsy?"

"No. What got us talking about it?" Betsy asked irritably.

"I did. Could you tell me," Nell asked, "whether Lady Laura—" She stopped. The name seemed to have had a strange effect on her audience. Charley's mouth had fallen open, and Betsy's had tightened until her lips were a thin, bitter line. She leaned forward and spoke slowly and menacingly.

"Nobody mentions that . . . that person in this place," she said. "Nobody. If you've got business up there, just keep it to yourself. We're not interested, see? If you want to know anything, don't ask here."

Charley found his voice.

"You know the old . . . you *know* her?" he asked Nell.

"Not yet."

"Then let me tell you something, friendly-like," he said. "If you go up that hill to Stapling, you'll get your feathers plucked. Nobody ever 'ad dealings with that . . . that person what you just mentioned, without coming out on the losing side. Ask anyone in Rivering. Ask Betsy. Betsy knows."

"And my father knows better than me," Betsy said bitterly. "Why d'you think he's never here? Because he's had enough, that's why. I don't say he was right to stick it out. If you ask me, I think he was wrong. Like I said just now, this place could do with a going-over. It's out of date. It's had its day. If we was one of those picture-postcard inns, like on the London road, a sort of roadhouse, then all right, we could have gone on doing good business—or anyway, business. But we weren't going to turn somersaults and turn the whole place upside down to make it the way *she* wanted it. My father owns this place, and his father and grandfather and great-grandfather and great-great-grandfather owned it before him, and it's always been the White Hart and it's always done all right, until that . . . who you said . . . came driving down here in her little rattletrap and started telling us what to do. If they'd been suggestions, then yes, we would have listened and given them our—our consideration. But no orders. We don't take orders not from her and not from anyone—not that sort of orders. 'We're honest yeoman stock,' that's what my dad told her, 'as old as your family and twice as useful. There are earls *and* earls,' he said, straight to her face. 'Some count and some don't and your lot never did, right from the beginning until they petered out.' 'I warn you,' she said to him, 'I warn you; this is your chance and I won't give you another so I advise you to take it.' So he didn't. That was Dad. If she'd gone about it the right way, he might . . . No. He wouldn't have done anything but what he did do. So we don't like people coming in here and mentioning that name. We don't bear grudges, at least Dad doesn't, but enough's enough. Charley, carry up that tray."

"No. I will. It isn't heavy," Nell said.

She picked it up and went to the door. Charley opened it and she went upstairs. A bell was ringing endlessly—Mrs. Saltry's, she presumed. She knocked at the door of her room and entered, to find her sitting up in bed with one finger on the bell.

"Oh, it's you, Nell. I've been ringing for hours. What's gone wrong with the service? And what's got into you, carry-ing trays around?"

"No service. Charley and Betsy are in the kitchen. Staff meals come before guest meals. I cooked bacon and eggs for myself, but I know you only take coffee." She put the tray on the bedside table and drew up a chair. "I'm having some with you. Did you sleep?"

"Some. I'd like to say I didn't, but I did. If you'd asked me if I was warm and comfortable, then no, I wasn't—but I did manage to get some sleep. How about you?"

Nell did not answer the question. After a few moments, she spoke thoughtfully.

"In the kitchen just now," she said, "I was going to ask them something—I forget exactly what—about Lady Laura. All I got out was her name. After that, Betsy did the talking. She warned me not to ever mention the name again."

"Whose? Lady Laura's?"

"Yes. Every time they had to use it, she and Charley, they didn't."

"What did she do to them, for heaven's sake?"

"I don't know. It was something to do with making over this place."

"It could do with making over."

"Betsy admitted that, but she said her father wouldn't take orders from . . . you know who. What's honest yeoman stock?"

"What's what?"

"Honest yeoman stock."

"Well, it's . . . they're those . . . You must have seen them at the Tower of London, dressed up in those hats?"

"I know, but what—" Nell broke off, put down her empty cup, and rose. "It doesn't matter. See you in an hour?"

"Yes. Are you going to call and tell the lawyer we're coming?"

Nell considered.

"No," she decided. "He might start fussing and making appointments. We'll just go and get it over with."

CHAPTER

4

"Are you sure we're going the right way?" Mrs. Saltry inquired an hour and a half later. "His office wouldn't be here, in a street like this."

"I looked at the town plan," Nell told her. "This is the way."

She was driving; the office was well within walking distance, but she had decided to take the car in case it was needed when she went up to the Manor. She turned into the cul-de-sac, slowed down to note the numbers and stopped outside the door with the gleaming brass plate.

"This is it," she said.

They got out of the car, and Mrs. Saltry looked disparagingly up and down the street.

"This district," she commented, "has come down in the world. Why hasn't he moved out?"

Nell made no answer. She was leading the way up the steps. In the narrow entrance she paused to study the directional signs.

"Not upstairs—that's dressmakers. And not down on that side—that's gardeners. Let's try here."

She knocked on the only remaining door, and received a courteous invitation to enter. She ushered Mrs. Saltry inside, and followed, closing the door behind her. Miss Dell, who was arranging her recently-begun stamp collection, rose to greet them.

"Good morning. May I offer you chairs? Mr. Brierley isn't in yet, but he won't be long. While waiting for him, I was putting my stamps into this little book. Do either of you ladies collect stamps?"

"No," Mrs. Saltry said. Her eyes, at first fixed in wonder on Miss Dell, were now taking in details of the room, and missing nothing—the dust, the disorder, the absence of any evidence that business, legal or otherwise, was ever transacted here. Through the half-open door that led to Cosmo's room she could see his desk, with its jumble of papers, yesterday's teacup, last week's crumpled newspapers. Her eyes came back to Miss Dell. How old? Sixty, seventy, eighty? Who could tell?

"I do wish," Mis Dell was saying, "that I had begun my stamp collection when I was younger. Not that it matters, because I haven't anybody like a nephew or anyone of that kind to whom I could leave it." Her eyes rested on Nell. "Have we met before, anywhere?" she asked.

"I don't think so."

"Your face seems extraordinarily familiar. I don't think you told me your name."

"Berg. I wrote to Mr. Brierley about two weeks ago."

"Oh, did you? You wrote, you say?"

"Yes. To tell him we'd be coming in to see him. I wrote from Paris."

"Paris?" Miss Dell's brows were knitted. "No, I don't think I remember . . . Paris, you said? In that case, it would be filed under *P*, wouldn't it?" She rose and went to a very large, new filing cabinet standing in a corner. She slid open the top drawer and there was a sound of rattling crockery. "The tea things," she explained. "In the middle of the morning, Mr. Brierley sometimes likes a hot cup of tea, so I keep the things ready. I used to keep them in that little cupboard, but this drawer is so much handier." She closed it, opened the one below, and lifted out a box of biscuits. "Would you care for one of these biscuits?" she asked. "I always keep them by me—the tin keeps them quite fresh."

Nell and Mrs. Saltry thanked her, but said they would not care for a biscuit. Miss Dell replaced the box, closed the drawer and resumed her seat.

"Now, what were we saying before I came across that box?" she asked.

"You were looking for a letter," Mrs. Saltry informed her. "A letter my cousin wrote from Paris."

"Your cousin? You have a cousin in Paris?"

"No. She's here, beside me. Miss Berg. She's the one who wrote to Mr. Brierley from Paris."

"As well as your cousin?"

"Miss Berg, Miss Ellen Berg is my cousin. She's the daughter—"

"Just one moment." Miss Dell held up a long, well-shaped hand. "Forgive me for interrupting, but I like to take things in order. I have a passion, a real passion for order. Now let us begin again. You have come to see Mr. Brierley, bringing your cousin Miss Berg with you. Your name is—?"

"Mrs. Saltry. But I don't want to see Mr. Brierley."

"You don't?"

"No. It's Miss Berg who wants to. Maybe Mr. Brierley isn't coming to work today?"

"Oh, yes—certainly he'll come," Miss Dell said with confidence. "If anything delays or prevents him, or if his car won't start, he always telephones."

"Does he have to come far? I mean, does he live right here in town?" Nell asked.

"No. He lives up on the hill, very close to the Manor. In fact, you might almost say that the house is part of the domain. I'm sure he won't be long, but before he arrives, perhaps I ought to take your measurements."

"Measurements? Measurements for what?" Mrs. Saltry inquired uneasily.

"Ah, *that's* what we've got to decide." Miss Dell gave her a winning smile. "We haven't really gone into it, have we? If you'll come upstairs, I'll show you my fashion books. They're not new, but my dear mother used to say: 'Keep any pattern ten years, and you'll find it's in fashion again.' How true that is! I must have known that I was to have customers today; why else would I have left my little snippets of material upstairs, ready for you to look through and choose what you would like? But you mustn't let my pre-knowledge surprise you. I am"—she leaned forward and lowered her voice—"psychic."

"Is that so?" Mrs. Saltry glanced nervously at the door. "That's very interesting, but maybe we'd better—"

"All my life," continued Miss Dell, "I used to astonish my mother—until she realized that I had the gift of second sight. I won't claim to be able to know *what* is going to happen, but I do know that *something* is going to happen. I am able to warn people. 'Don't go out today,' I tell them. 'Stay indoors and you will be safe.' Many a time my sisters have been grateful to me for saving them from something that would have harmed them."

"Such as what?" Mrs. Saltry asked with mounting interest.

"Well, if they had gone out, they would have found out—but they listened to my warning, and stayed at home on that particular day or days, and so of course they avoided knowing what. I see danger as a kind of shadow." Her eyes remained fixed at a point above Mrs. Saltry's head, and Mrs. Saltry looked up uneasily. "A black shadow. When I see it hovering over somebody, I know that person is going to be in some kind of trouble—perhaps even danger."

"And you warn them?" Mrs. Saltry asked, now deeply interested.

"I do. It is my clear duty. If they refuse to believe me, that is their own affair, their own risk. There is a shadow above you now, this minute, but only a slight one."

Mrs. Saltry stared at her. "Over *me?*"

"Yes. As I said, slight."

"So I should have stayed home?"

"How could you? You have only just heard of it. As soon as you came into the room, I *felt* something. It was—"

She stopped. Another shadow had fallen, this time on the square of glass in the door. The handle turned. Cosmo came in, turned to close the door behind him, and froze before the movement was completed. For some moments he remained motionless, his eyes on Nell. Then he spoke quietly.

"My dear, how like, how very like your mother you are."

Nell smiled—a slow, lovely smile—and put out her hand. He came forward and took it in both of his. Nell turned to present him to Mrs. Saltry, but Miss Dell spoke first.

"No, no, Mr. Brierley. These ladies are not mother and daughter," she explained. "They are cousins. One is called Mrs. Saltry, and the other—"

"—is called Ellen Berg. I know," said Cosmo, smiling. "And you should have known too, Miss Dell, by Miss Berg's likeness to her mother, Lady Helen. Lady Laura is her great-aunt."

Miss Dell stared at him. Then two red patches appeared on her cheeks and spread slowly inward, until they were checked by the formidable nasal barrier. She spoke with an effort. "I am glad I didn't know that," she said. "I should have found it difficult to remain here until your arrival. Please explain to Miss Berg that I have nothing against her, but I cannot hear her great-aunt's name spoken in my presence without . . . without—"

"That's all right," Nell broke in. "You're not the only

one. Every time I've spoken it, I've stirred up something. Mrs. Saltry is my cousin, third or fourth," she went on to explain to Cosmo. "She's been travelling with me."

"And I guess this is where I stop travelling," Mrs. Saltry said. "Nell wants to talk with you and I guess you've a lot to say to her, so I'll stay here with Miss Dell till you're through, or maybe I'll go for a drive. The car's just outside. If you don't need Miss Dell, maybe she could come too, and show me around?"

"That would be an excellent idea," Cosmo said. "But . . . did you say your car was outside?"

"Yes. The little blue number."

"In this street?"

"Yes. We left it—" she broke off and gave a cry. "Ernie Lauder!"

She went to the door, wrenched it open and rushed outside. She returned a few moments later, and spoke through set teeth.

"If there's justice in this town," she told Cosmo, "I'm going to have Ernie Lauder carved into pieces and broiled. If it's promotion he's after, I'll get him promoted all the way to Chenco, Arizona, where I keep a gun and know how to use it." She picked up her handbag. "Isn't there some big chief I could go to," she asked, "to tell him this Ernie Lauder is persecuting two harmless lady tourists? Yesterday, when the car hadn't been outside the White Hart more than a couple of minutes, it disappeared. And today, when Miss—Miss— when your secretary's a witness that we weren't in here more than a few minutes, this Ernie Lauder makes it vanish again."

"He was the shadow," Miss Dell said.

Mrs. Saltry turned to stare at her. "He was the what?"

"Didn't I tell you I saw a shadow over you? That must have been at the very moment when the car was being towed away. And now I'm afraid you'll have to go and get it back."

"I'll go," Nell said.

"No, not you. Me," Mrs. Saltry told her. "I'll walk to that square and pick up a cab and go and get the car, and then I'll drive it right over Ernie Lauder's body. And after that, I'll go up and meet you at Mr. Brierley's house."

"My . . . my house?" Cosmo said, aghast.

"Didn't Miss Dell tell me your house was practically part of the Manor? Did I get it wrong?" Mrs. Saltry asked him.

"No, but—"

"Well then, you and Nell can talk all you want to right here, and after that won't you be taking her up to see the ruin, and Lady . . . I mean, to see the Manor? While you're doing that, I'll sit in your house, if your wife will let me, and wait for Nell."

"I have no wife, but—"

"Then can someone let me into the house?"

He heard himself explaining that the door was never locked.

"Fine. Then I wait there, and you go with Nell to see . . . you go with Nell. Goodbye, Miss Dell. Maybe we can have our drive some other time."

Cosmo accompanied her out to the street, giving her far from clear directions as to how she could get to his house. Then he walked slowly back to his office. Miss Dell had taken Nell to a chair beside his desk and then withdrew ceremoniously, leaving the two alone.

When Cosmo was settled in his chair, Nell smiled at him.

"It's been a long time," she said.

"Yes, a long, long time," he agreed.

"Were you surprised to get my letter from Paris?"

"I was more than surprised. I was alarmed."

"Alarmed? What was there to be alarmed about?"

"That I shall explain presently. You wrote in your letter, Nell—I may call you Nell?—that you knew nothing about the Manor until after your father died. I knew that he had decided to tell you nothing, but I hoped he would change his mind. Did he never—"

(74)

"He didn't say one word, ever, about anything to do with the Manor. I knew my mother had been born in a kind of historic house in England, but nothing ever came up about her being the owner—or, after her, me. When my father died and I was going through everything, there was this little steel box with a key tied to it. I opened it and found all there was to find—your letters to my mother after she left here, hers to you saying she'd never come back while her aunt was alive, your letter telling about the bombs and the Manor being a ruin . . ." She paused. "I guess that's why my father didn't say anything. If all there was left was a ruin, he must have said to himself that there was no hurry to tell me about it."

"Didn't he tell you anything about your mother's past?"

"He told me all I ever wanted to know, but I guess I didn't ask much—she'd been dead since I was three, and I didn't think about her very often. Mrs. Saltry filled in about my father being sent to Rivering, and falling in love, and how her aunt did all she could to break it up. Nothing about earls or titles, nothing about my mother's real name, was ever mentioned by my father. You knew from what my mother wrote to you that she never wanted to be anything but plain Mrs. Matthew Berg."

"Yes, I knew."

"When I found those letters in the box, and read them, I started straight off to write to you, but then I thought maybe it would be better to let it sink in, take it slowly, think about it. Then I decided to come to England and see you and the ruin. Corinne—Mrs. Saltry—thought I ought to take in Europe while I was at it, and she offered to come, too. So we came"—she hesitated—"and then, well, I found I didn't know anything, and I started to learn, and I guess I went on too long, and didn't write to you. In Paris, Corinne made me write, and . . . here I am. What did Lady Laura say when you told her?"

There was a pause. Cosmo had turned slightly in his chair

and was staring out at the shabby street; he seemed to be trying to remember exactly what Lady Laura had said. Then he turned and faced Nell. "I didn't tell her," he said.

In the silence that followed, some undisturbed part of his mind saluted her for the way in which she sat quietly turning over the possibilities.

"She's kind of old, and can't take shocks?" she hazarded.

"No, she's in splendid health."

"She hated my mother, so she didn't want to hear about me?"

"She and your mother . . . they certainly didn't get on well. But the reason I didn't tell her, Nell, was simply that I couldn't bring myself to. Let me try to explain, and don't judge me too harshly. I am not a brave man. I've never been in a position to test my physical courage, but I am certainly a moral coward; I have never been able to stand up to Lady Laura. When your mother was here, I had very little to do with the Manor, very little business to transact. Your mother saw to everything, and at the time she became engaged to your father, he and she dealt with Lady Laura and I had nothing to do with any of their arrangements. It was not until the end of the war that it became necessary for me to assume my duties as a trustee. And when I did, I realized at once I was no match for Lady Laura. She made plans, I protested; she took absolutely no notice of anything I said, merely proceeding as if I had no right to interfere. For nearly thirty years, Lady Laura has overridden my protests, and has gone her own way. You have come to see a ruin, and certainly part of the Manor is a ruin—but that is not all you are going to see. May I outline the picture of what has been happening?"

"Please."

"When your mother went away, Lady Laura realized that she was probably going to live the rest of her life alone, and she decided that she would make herself as comfortable as she could. She moved almost at once into the solar wing and . . ."

"The what?"

"Medieval manor houses were built on a very simple plan. There was a large central hall, and on one side of this were the kitchens and the family bedrooms. On the other side was the solar, or ladies' retiring or withdrawing rooms. The solar usually had cellars and storerooms below it. The solar of Stapling Manor was in better preservation than any other part of the building. As I said, Lady Laura moved there— and it was as well she did, for shortly afterwards, bombs destroyed most of the rest of the Manor. The outer walls were in most places left standing, but the inside was wrecked. After the bombs fell, Lady Laura was greatly helped by the Americans stationed down at Rivering. They assembled the stones from the Manor to fill up a gap that had been made in the wall surrounding the Manor. In the gap, she built three small houses. I live in one of them. One of the bombs made a huge crater, and this is now a lake. There are tenants in all three houses, and the riding stables have been restored and let to the wife of the man who lives in the house next door to mine. The summerhouse is let to an archaeologist—he also rents the third house, but he doesn't spend much time in it. The day your letter came from Paris, I was very much upset; it was he who suggested that perhaps you would change your mind about coming here, and that I might postpone telling Lady Laura."

He stopped. She remained silent for what seemed to him a very long time. He traced a pattern in the dust of his desk and tried to keep his eyes away from her; looking at her took him back to a part of his past which he found painful. There was nothing in her voice or her manner that recalled her mother; only when he saw her face did his heart contract.

"You mean," she said at last, "that Lady Laura would have been upset if you'd told her about my letter, because of having to explain why she did all this when she wasn't the owner?"

Cosmo stared at her helplessly. "It wasn't to spare her feelings that I said nothing about your letter, Nell. I'm sorry to tell you she wouldn't have been at all upset. What your letter did was bring home to me my position. Not only had I failed to stop her from doing all these things; I hadn't even had the courage to write to your mother or your father to tell them what was going on."

"They made it clear, didn't they, that they didn't want to know?"

"Yes, but they should have wanted to know—and I should have told them."

"So you're upset because she's been making a lot of money and not handing any of it over to me?"

"I am aware, Nell, that you don't need money. But that doesn't alter the situation. Even if you had needed it desperately, you wouldn't have been given any of it. Lady Laura, from the moment your mother left, considered the Manor and its grounds her own. She has acted all these years as she would have done if she had actually been the owner. After what I've told you, it will be hard for you to believe that I am not afraid of her. What I am afraid of, what I have a dread of, is meeting in anybody the kind of ruthlessness which Lady Laura has, which doesn't manifest itself in loud words or violent actions, but is simply like a flood or an avalanche, sweeping away everything that's in its way."

"Has she been doing some sweeping at the White Hart?"

"Did they say anything?"

"They won't hear her name mentioned. Why not?"

"She organized summer showings of *son et lumière,* and arranged with travel agents in various towns within a reasonable distance to bring coachloads of spectators to the Manor. She wanted the White Hart to provide a meal—not a full-scale dinner, but a cold snack, perhaps a buffet. The proprietor refused to do it. He would have agreed to some kind of compromise if he had been given time, but Lady Laura doesn't give second chances. She settled the matter by putting the money up for the renovation of the hotel opposite the White Hart, so that they would provide meals for coachloads who wanted them. The White Hart will lose a lot of business."

"I see. A farmer—he looked like a farmer—last night at dinner called her an old witch. What had she done to him?"

"He was probably Enoch Wright. He rented some land near the lake and went to great trouble and expense to build up a business in cut flowers. When he had got it onto a paying basis, Lady Laura turned him out and ran the business herself."

"And what did she do to Miss Dell?"

"Miss Dell's mother was a dressmaker. She and her three daughters lived and worked on the floor above this one. Lady Laura put them out of business by financing a rival establishment. There are many others who don't like to hear her name mentioned. She will tell you that she gave all these people a chance to cooperate, and they refused to take it."

"I'll have to go and see her, won't I?"

"Yes. I'll drive you up in my car."

She glanced at the telephone. "Maybe we should call her, to see if she's there?"

"We shall know as soon as we get inside the grounds. She flies a pennant to show whether she's in or out."

Nell laughed. "Like royalty?"

"Yes. But the idea is a practical one. All Lady Laura's ideas are very practical indeed." He got up and walked to the door and opened it. "I shall take you to her, and—"

"No. I'll drive up there with you, but I think I'd like to go in myself. Shall I have to tell her about writing a letter?"

Cosmo smiled. "I'm afraid you'll have to. She will hardly believe that you—"

"—just dropped by? Then I'll say what's true, that I wrote you a letter but didn't say exactly when I was coming, and as I didn't sound too sure about coming, you didn't say anything." She paused for a few moments. "You needn't think," she went on slowly, "that all this—I mean my aunt going around doing everything she wanted to do—is your fault. I guess it's really my father's. He knew about what she was like—he must have known. He must have known all these years that she was still alive and still raising the dust, but all he told you was not to bother letting him know anything. He just put the whole thing up on a shelf for the next twenty years. I don't blame him. I can see why he and my mother didn't count on coming back while Lady Laura was still here. All the same, leaving you on your own didn't help much, did it?"

She walked past him and paused to say goodbye to Miss Dell.

"Oh, not goodbye. Now that you're here," Miss Dell protested, "you mustn't run away again. I shall take you upstairs next time you come to see Mr. Brierley, and show you the very room in which your mother used to have her fittings for her party frocks when she was a little girl."

"Thank you. I'd like that," Nell said.

The garage in which Cosmo left his car was not far away. As they walked to it, he gave fervent thanks that this was the day on which the car received its monthly cleaning. It did not look smart as he drove it out into the street to pick up Nell, but he felt that there was no need to be ashamed of it.

He drove slowly at first, pointing out to her any buildings which had any connection with her parents. Then the town came to an end and the road curved towards the hillside. They passed the signpost, and then there was nothing to see but woodland until at last the ancient wall came into view. It was broken by a beautiful arch, and beneath this Cosmo drove.

"You're home," he said. "Welcome."

"Thank you." They drove slowly over the bridge and then along the winding beech avenue. Ahead, Nell could see a chimney and a fluttering pennant—no more. And then Cosmo drove round the last curve and stopped the car.

"There it is," he said quietly.

She could only gaze, speechless. She had expected to see a ruin, but this was a whole building, beautiful, untouched. Time seemed to rush backward, leaving her with a feeling of dizziness. She felt that she was gazing at a tapestry, like those which had hung in the galleries through which she had lately, endlessly walked. Her eyes followed the lovely lines, and she felt a pulse beating in her throat. The picture was one of utter peace. No sounds, except bird songs, disturbed it.

She spoke at last with difficulty. "I didn't know . . . I didn't expect . . ."

"I told you the walls were standing. Behind them, except in the restored solar wing, there is nothing—emptiness. But it was the fact that the façade remained so apparently untouched that made Lady Laura decide to organize the *son et lumière* displays. They are very popular, because—as you can see—this is a building peculiarly suited to them."

"Yes, I can see."

"You are sure you want to go in and see her alone?"

"Yes."

He got out and opened the door on her side. "You'll find an iron bell-pull beside the porch. You will be admitted by an old man called Banks, who was once your mother's chauffeur. His daughter works for Lady Laura too, and so does his son, who is part groom and part handyman."

"Groom?"

"No horses. Just a pony which pulls the governess cart in which Lady Laura goes about—that is, goes about the estate, or goes down into Rivering. When she goes up to London, which she does twice a month, she hires a car with a chauffeur."

"I'm glad she's got servants. I kind of wondered if she would have. It's not all that easy, is it?"

"Getting servants? No. But Lady Laura's will never leave her." He smiled. "It would be nice to think that they stayed with her because she treats them with kindness and consideration—but she doesn't. Mrs. Moulton, the lady who lives in the house next door to mine, is unable to understand why her once-a-week women, so well-paid and so indulged, leave constantly, while Lady Laura's staff remains, helping her to live in a style which most of us have come to regard as out-of-date. Would you like me to bring the car to fetch you?"

"No, thank you. How can I get to your house?"

"By taking that road over there, which leads to the lake. You'll see the summerhouse; the gate leading out of the grounds is quite close to it. Once you leave the grounds, you'll see the three little houses on your left, a few hundred yards away."

He stood watching as she walked out of the sunshine into the deep shade of the porch. Then he drove away. He stopped the car outside his garage, but made no move to get out; he sat dreaming of the past. How unexpected, how extraordinary, he thought, that she had brought back the past so vividly. How could he have dreamed that when he walked into his office this morning he would see . . .

He came abruptly out of his musings. He had seen two women in his office—and one was on her way to his house. She might be here at any moment.

He scrambled out of the car and went with all the speed he could muster into the house. He closed the front door and went frenziedly to work, removing last night's supper dishes, carrying piles of newspapers to the fireplace in the drawing room and pushing them up the chimney, stumbling with armfuls of books from the sofas and chairs on which they had lain, and hiding them in the boot cupboard. He found a carpet brush and fell on his knees and attempted to remove dust and crumbs from carpet and rugs. He looked in vain for a duster, but found in the kitchen an old shirt which he used as a substitute. From the downstairs cloakroom he snatched his slippers, his scattered shaving gear and a bundle of unwashed linen. He went up a few stairs and then turned and came down again, remembering that there would be no need for visitors to go up. And they would not need to enter the kitchen, so that he could spend what time remained in removing the mud from the floor of the hall. He hesitated between sweeping or using a damp cloth, decided on a damp cloth and had done no more than trace some dirt-streaked patterns across the tiles when he heard a car stop at the gate. He threw the cloth into the kitchen, pulled down his jacket, ran his hands over his hair to smooth it, waited to get his breath and then opened the door.

"You see, I got here." Mrs. Saltry spread her hands to take in the houses, the woods, the sunshine. "It's all so beautiful," she said.

"Won't you come in?"

"I had to pay another fine." Mrs. Saltry, to his infinite relief, talked her way through hall and drawing room and was still talking when he drew forward a chair. "Did Nell go and see Lady Laura by herself?"

"Yes. It was her own idea."

"She does have her own ideas. Have you found that out yet?"

"No."

"You will. Lady Laura will, too. Or she would if Nell was planning to stay for a while, which I hope she isn't. Mr.

Brierley, at this time of day, I can always use a drink. Do you have one?"

"A . . ." He stopped, a look of such distress on his face that she put an apprehensive question.

"You're not a teetotaler by any chance, are you?"

"Tee . . . oh no, no, no. It's just that—"

He broke off. There was beer, he remembered distractedly, and there was cider—several bottles of cider. There was soda water and Vichy water and good tap water and somewhere— he thought in his bedroom, where he had left it last time he had taken a tablespoon to cure a stomach-ache—there was a small, very small, bottle of brandy. But what he lacked, the Moultons would have. He seldom visited them, but he knew they had a cupboard in their dining room in which there was an impressive array of bottles. He had never borrowed anything from them before, but this was—wasn't it?—a kind of emergency.

"What would you like?" he asked.

"Well, that depends on what you've got. Martini? Gin and tonic?"

"Of course. Anything, anything . . . Please excuse me."

He closed the drawing room door carefully and tiptoed out of the house. Once outside, he broke into a trot. His laboured breathing was caused partly by the unaccustomed exercise, but also by fear that Mr. Moulton would be out. Mrs. Moulton would certainly not be at home—she left for the riding stables before he went to his office—but Mr. Moulton's day began in the afternoon, and he was usually in the house until lunch time.

He arrived at their front door and rang the bell. To his relief, he heard sounds within. One of the windows of the upper floor opened, and Mr. Moulton, in a fluffy bathrobe, leaned out.

"Oh, it's you, Cosmo. Not working today?"

"No. I have a visitor, visitors. A lady. An American lady.

She's in my house, in the drawing room. She would like a drink, but all I have . . . Would you most kindly allow me to borrow a bottle of Martini and a bottle of gin and a bottle, perhaps two bottles of tonic water? I will, of course, return full bottles at the first possible—"

He stopped. Mr. Moulton had withdrawn his head. A short time later the front door opened and he handed Cosmo two large and two small bottles.

"Aren't you rather going it, Cosmo?" he asked. "Did you say one lady, or two?"

"One. Another is coming. Thank you very much, very much indeed."

He backed away and then turned and hurried to his house, leaving Mr. Moulton looking after him with what, on any other countenance, would have been wistfulness. He muttered as he went: Glasses, glasses, glasses, ice, ice. No, there was no ice; he had forgotten to put water into the ice trays. Were there any clean glasses? If so, where? Try the dining room first, and if they were all used, wash one or two quickly, very quickly . . . she would be wondering what had happened to him.

What Mrs. Saltry was wondering was how a man with a skin as fresh as a baby's could keep his health when he was constantly breathing in dust flavoured with cheese, onions and beer. Who looked after him? Didn't anybody ever come in and clean up? Didn't anyone care? He was so gentle, so helpless, so alone. Ten years—hadn't he said, seeing her off from his office, that it was ten years—since his wife died? Hadn't anybody lifted a finger to help him in all that time? A pair of muddy boots was wedged under the sofa, the mud so dry that heaven only knew how long they had lain there. Every single picture crooked—she got up and straightened them—the sofa and chair-covers with gaping holes, three pairs of socks pushed behind a cushion that she had attempted to punch into shape. How could he live like this and look so well, so uncomplaining? If there was one thing she couldn't stand, it was to see old men, even not-so-old men, left on their own. A woman alone could always manage somehow—but a man couldn't. A man needed a woman. Even if he didn't need her as a bedfellow, he needed her for company, for cooking, for cleaning. She had never, she reminded herself, been able to stand those women who pounded typewriters and talked hot air about women's rights and fell down on the greatest right of all—looking after a man and bringing up his children, if any. You could see, just by looking, that this Cosmo was comfort-loving; look at his chessmen and his funny old-fashioned little radio and his bag of barley sugars at his elbow on that little table, and look at the little table, all white rings where he'd put his glass down all wet. Speaking of wet, was he going to bring those drinks, or shouldn't she go out there and find where he was and see if she couldn't do something to help him, or at least hurry him up.

She met Cosmo in the hall carrying a laden tray, and he broke into stumbling apologies for the absence of ice.

"Who cares about ice?" Mrs. Saltry, at his request, mixed her own drink and carried the glass to her chair. "Aren't you going to fix yourself a drink?"

"Yes, I will, of course. I think perhaps beer." But the beer had been hidden behind the bookshelf. "No, just a little tonic water."

"You don't have a slice of lemon, do you?" she asked.

"Lemon?" He splashed tonic water on the tray, put down the bottle and went to the door. "Of course, I should have remembered. A slice of lemon. Will you excuse me?"

Mr. Moulton, this time in shirt-sleeves at the bedroom window, came down and gave him two lemons, together with some good-natured advice on avoiding over-excitement. But Cosmo scarcely heard it; he hurried back to his house, crept in cautiously and went to the kitchen to slice the lemons. He put the slices onto a saucer and went back to the drawing room, and Mrs. Saltry looked with remorse at his moist brow.

"I'm giving you a lot of trouble," she said. "Sit down and relax. I've got everything I want. I'll get you that tonic water—no, sit down, sit down and let me do it. And I'm going to put in just a drop of gin."

He cooled down by degrees and found himself enjoying more every minute the unaccustomed scene—himself taking his ease in the middle of the morning in his own drawing room; a charming, elegant woman seated in his own comfortable armchair, giving a touch of sophistication to the homely room, talking in her light voice with its pretty accent, telling him about Chenco and the ranch, and what Nell did there; describing her own beautiful house with its spacious patio, her two coloured maids named Tessie and Blanche, and the swimming pool built to look like a natural lake, with lovely trees to shade it and a sunny bank if you wanted to lie there and get an all-over tan. It all sounded very different from Rivering.

"But you have to get out of Chenco every so often, Cosmo —you said I could call you Cosmo, didn't you? Chenco's fine if you can leave it maybe once or twice a year and freshen up, breathe new air, take a look at what's going on outside. My husband, the first one, didn't agree with that. He liked to stay home, and that's what broke it up in the end, the way he wouldn't move because he said he didn't see any point in fixing his home so's it was comfortable, and then leaving it to go and be uncomfortable in places he didn't find as interesting as the one he'd left behind. How it was, he got to be too dependent on his friends. Maybe you don't know this, but American men like to get together. So do Englishmen—I know that, because my second husband was English —but Englishmen get together to play games, or kill things, or keep themselves in good physical shape; they don't just get together to drink to their college days, or if they do, I never saw them at it. That was a thing Nell's father never did and never would do. He . . . but why am I telling you? You knew him. He was here. Did you kind of get friendly?"

"Well, not exactly. We met, strangely enough, at the White Hart. I was in charge of the Rivering Home Guard and we had our headquarters in the hotel opposite, which had been requisitioned. I went across one evening to arrange something with the White Hart landlord, but he was out, and I had to wait, so I sat in the bar and the only other man in it was an American. We began to talk, and . . ." Cosmo's voice slowed as the years rolled backward. "The most extraordinary thing was that it was through me that he met Nell's mother."

"No, *really?*"

"Yes. She came down one day to see me—she used to come into my office and have a talk with me whenever things up at the Manor got too much for her."

"You mean whenever she and her aunt had a fight?"

"You could put it like that; yes. One day, when she came, we met by chance in the square. Nell's father came out of the White Hart, where some of the Americans were billeted, and—"

"—saw her and that was it?"

"Yes. I had never, until then, believed that it was possible for a man and a woman to see one another for the first time and . . . and know that they had fallen in love, but I believed it then, because I saw it happen before my eyes. She was standing beside me. He stood looking at her from across the square, and then he walked slowly towards us. When he got close to us, I told her who he was, and I told him who she was. He said—and I remember that he said it unsmilingly—'Hello, Helen,' and she . . ."

"Go on. She—?"

"She didn't say anything. She put out a hand—not in the

way you put out a hand for a handshake. He took it and held it. I stayed there for a little while and tried to make conversation, but I realized they weren't listening. I liked to remember those moments afterwards, when Lady Laura was doing her best to drive a wedge between them."

"How do you go about driving a wedge between two people in that state of mind, if mind comes into it?"

"By pointing out, at every possible opportunity, how unsuitable a marriage between them would be. By hinting to his superior officers that he was making a nuisance of himself. By refusing to leave him alone with her, so that they were driven to meeting wherever else they could. Usually, they met in the rooms I had in the town."

Mrs. Saltry got up and poured herself another drink.

"That doesn't sound like Matthew Berg," she commented, back in her chair. "The way I knew him, he would have taken just so much of Lady Laura and then—pff, suddenly —no more. He was . . . well, you only have to look at Nell to know what I mean. Calm. Kind of placid, and with a lot of sense. Horse sense. When you said just now that her mother used to go down and let off steam in your office, I could see her doing it—but Nell wouldn't act that way. Most of the things you think are going to make her angry just make her laugh—but when she does go overboard, she goes and that's what her father used to do. No warning—just the take-off, so you got a nasty shock. Nell likes to take her own time. You can't hurry her, so it's no use trying. After reading those letters after her father died, she took her time making up her mind what she'd do—about coming over here, I mean. She certainly took her time on the way. She's taken in enough history and what goes with it to last her the rest of her life."

"Does she run her father's ranch?"

"It's not her father's any more; it's hers, and she doesn't run it and I don't think she ever will. Matthew must have taken it hard, but he didn't say much. He lined up all the promising young ranchers he could find, hoping she'd marry one of them and settle down on the place—one of the ones he lined up was my own son, Jack. But Nell wouldn't have any one of them—including Jack. Matthew Berg put a clause in his will saying that if ever Nell wanted to leave the ranch, he'd like Jack to stay and take over. He's staying anyway; Nell's put him there for keeps with a quarter share, which is more than he's worth at this minute, though he'll grow into it. What Nell wants to do, or where she wants to go, is anybody's guess. All I hope is, all I pray is that she won't want to stay here. I don't mean here in Rivering; I mean here in England. I didn't like the way she looked in London."

"How she—?"

"She looked at home. In all those other places, Paris and Rome and the others, she was just a tourist. She dug deeper than most, but she was still a tourist. In London, she . . . well, she was different. Don't ask me how she was different, or how different she was, because I wouldn't be able to explain. When it comes to guessing what people don't want to tell you, I'm lost—but certainly in London, she had a look of belonging, and I didn't like it. I'm not going to say one word against the English, because sometimes you meet one of them you like right away, like you, but as a race, and as husbands, you can have them." She handed her glass to Cosmo for refilling. "This talk I've had with you," she told him, "is the first real pleasure I've had since we got to this country. I can't tell you how nice it is to sit here and just relax and look out at that lovely view."

Cosmo thought it a pity that humans could not purr; never had he felt more like purring than at this moment. He would have shrunk in alarm or distaste from the slightest hint of coyness or insincerity or archness in his visitor's voice or manner, but she was, he saw with pleasure, at ease, at home, speaking in sensible, matter-of-fact tones, enjoying herself in the most natural way in the world. He could not remember when he had enjoyed himself so much.

"Any time you want to come up here and use this house," he heard himself saying, "please do so. I am at my office all day, and only get home at six o'clock. Please come up here whenever you like. The front door is never locked."

"That's nice and thoughtful of you," Mrs. Saltry said. "I'll be sure to come. There's nowhere down in that White Hart I could stay, and until Nell gets through with whatever she plans to do here, I'll be glad to accept your offer. But why don't you give yourself a vacation while we're here? It won't be for long. Why don't you let Miss Dell take care of the customers, and stay home for a week or so?"

He looked at her with increasing respect and admiration. "You know, Mrs. Saltry, I—"

"Corinne."

"You know, Corinne, that might be an excellent plan. I could see so much more of Nell, and of you, and—"

"Then it's settled. You're on your vacation. Tell me something: your Miss Dell—is she psychic, like she says?"

"Miss Dell?"

"Yes. All those shadows she sees—does she just make them up?"

Cosmo hesitated. "I would find it difficult," he said at last, "to recall any occasion on which she has actually, as it were, foretold an occurrence, an event. But she has a strange, very disturbing way of knowing or guessing when people are going to—"

"—run into trouble?"

"Yes. She isn't taken seriously, I'm afraid, but there have certainly been times when the shadows she claims to have seen—"

"—have turned into Ernie Lauder?"

"Have turned into some kind of misfortune. Most people think it has been merely coincidence."

"And what do you think?"

"She is a very truthful person; I am quite sure she wouldn't make false claims. If she sees shadows, they are there—but if they are there, and nobody but Miss Dell can see them, it—"

"—puts her in the witch bracket. Or racket. You kind of look after her, don't you?"

"I employ her."

"Because nobody else would. Did anybody ever tell you you were a very nice man?"

"I don't think so."

"Then I'm telling you now," she said.

CHAPTER

5

As Nell walked into the shelter of the porch and stood before the massive doorway, she had an unsettling impression that she was entering a fortress. The walls looked not only incredibly thick, but gave her a feeling of timelessness that brought to her mind the brevity of her allotment of three-score years and ten. But when she stepped backward and glanced to her left, the illusion of strength and age was shattered, for she could see clearly the emptiness that lay behind the beautiful façade—a shell, open to the sky, held upright in places by iron supports.

She seized the bell-pull and gave it a tug and heard from somewhere inside the building its hollow summons. Footsteps sounded, and then the rattle of bolts—perhaps it was a fortress, after all? The door was opened by an old man who had an air of weary dignity; when his eyes fell on her, she thought a gleam of recognition or speculation lit his gaze, but his grave manner did not change.

"Good morning. Would you ask Lady Laura if she would see me, please? My name is Miss Ellen Berg."

He bowed, opened the door wider, closed it behind her and led her with slow, stately steps across a wide, flagged hall and up four shallow steps to an arched doorway. He opened the door and ushered her inside and she saw that she was in a dark, immensely long drawing room. The man-servant invited her to be seated, and walking to a door half-way down the room, opened it and disappeared. Reappearing after an interval, he informed her that Lady Laura would be with her in a moment, and then went away, his footsteps echoing down the four steps to the hall.

Nell stood and looked round her. Her ability to recognize or to date furniture was, she knew, so slight as to be non-existent, but she sensed that the contents of the room were of great age and of great value. She felt like a tourist in a museum, and knew that if she stayed much longer, waiting, she would get a walled-in feeling; the windows were high, and set deep in the walls; there was no view, not much air, and hardly any light. Nothing in the room suggested that this was anybody's home; she thought it grand, but lifeless.

She saw with relief a piece of furniture that gave her a reassuring sense of familiarity—a desk with a block front exactly like one which had stood in her father's room, and which he had told her was copied by the furniture makers of Newport and Philadelphia from an English design. She went up to it and, standing beside it, found herself recovering from her brief sense of having lost her identity.

How long was a moment? Why didn't Lady Laura come?

She entered almost soundlessly; only a faint rustle told Nell that she was in the room—and when she turned and looked at her, a faint hope within her died—the hope that she would perhaps prove to be just like any other old lady, an old lady who could be anybody's aunt or great-aunt, an old lady like the ones to be seen every day in the library at Chenco, neat and trim and bespectacled and down-to-earth. This was not, she saw at once, any old lady. Tall, thin, dressed in a gray, softly-draped material and wearing—why, for goodness' sake?—a hat, small, toque-like, with folds of the same colour as the dress, folds of some gauzy, lace-like fabric, covering the brim. Not just an old lady. A chatelaine. A long, silver-knobbed stick. And beautiful. Smooth gray hair, high cheekbones, a small nose and eyes that were clear and blue—and probing.

They faced one another across the room. Lady Laura had closed the door by which she had entered, but she had not moved away from it; she paused to study Nell. And Nell was unaware that that long, searching gaze was one which she herself always directed at strangers. This silent interval was one which always preceded her own opening remarks.

She heard a low, slow, calm, languid voice. "Banks recognized you, of course." She was approaching; she stopped a few paces away. "Anyone who had known your mother would know you at sight. He said your name was Ellen. Perhaps he meant to say Helen?"

"No. It's Ellen. I'm called Nell."

"Sit down, please. Over there."

Nell sat, and as she did so, she called up her reserves. The voice and the manner were challenging enough, but she thought she could deal with those; what she was beginning to detect, and what she feared, was the quality that had defeated Cosmo Brierley, that he had found impossible to combat—an ironclad assurance that was above and beyond arrogance, a calm superiority which was daunting because it was entirely natural, entirely unassumed.

Lady Laura had seated herself on a high-backed chair. "How long have you been in England?" she inquired.

"About two weeks. We came over—"

"We?"

"A cousin came over with me. She's a widow, about fifty, and she—"

"Why didn't you write to tell me you were coming?"

(95)

"I wrote to Mr. Brierley, but all I told him was that we were in Paris and might be taking a trip to see the . . . the ruin. That's what I thought the Manor was—just a ruin. My letter was kind of vague, so he—"

"My dear Ellen, it would perhaps be better not to begin by distorting facts. If you wrote to Cosmo Brierley, he should have shown me the letter, however vague. The reason he didn't do so is that he undoubtedly became panic-stricken at the thought of your arrival. He has lived in dread of it for years. He took full advantage of your father's decision to keep you in ignorance of your mother's family history, by telling you nothing of the changes I was making here. He is a pusillanimous and spineless old man, quite unfit to manage his own or anybody else's affairs. When did you write?"

"I forget." Nell spoke with as much calm as she could summon. "And I don't know about pusi . . . about spineless, but when I met him today, I thought he was very nice and very kind."

"He is far from nice in the sense in which the word was once used; it once meant fastidious. He is not likely to take you to his house, but if he did, you would discover that he is very far from nice. He was married for ten years to a woman of strong character who did her best to raise him to a higher level of niceness, and while she lived, she had a measure of success. When she died, he reverted at once to his former lamentable state. I cannot understand how he ever came to be a lawyer. Lawyers frequently assume, as he assumed, a position as trustee, and should have a grasp of what their responsibilities entail. As trustee here, he has been completely useless."

"Isn't that because you wouldn't listen to anything he said?"

Lady Laura, upright and motionless, one hand on her lap, the other on the knob of the walking stick, studied her for some moments.

"If he told you that," she said at last, "he must also have told you something about the changes I have made on the estate. If I had not made them, you would have found here nothing but what you expected to find—a ruined Manor house, one part of its surrounding wall destroyed, the moat drained and a huge crater torn in the grounds. If I had not made the first change—moving into the solar wing when your mother went away—I should either have been killed by a bomb, or made homeless." She rose, walked to the fireplace and pulled a bell-rope. "There is time before luncheon to take you round and show you what I have done. I cannot walk far. I have a governess cart with a pony and I use it in the grounds and when I go down to Rivering. I go down seldom; I prefer the townspeople to come to me. That is why I arranged to fly a signal to indicate whether I was at home or not; it can be seen from the lower road, and saves Banks the trouble of dealing with a succession of people who come to see me on business, and have to be sent away again. I have no social contacts except those—like this one —which are unavoidable. I have a great deal of business to see to, and I will not have people wasting my time. Banks," she instructed the old man, who had come in answer to her summons, "please tell Vincent I want the trap at once."

"Very good, m'lady." Banks withdrew, and Nell wondered how many times a day he had to come in answer to the bell, and why no word had been said of who she was. In surroundings like these, she decided, friendly exchanges must long ago have become frozen.

"How much," Lady Laura asked, still standing by the fireplace, "do you know about furniture?"

"Almost nothing at all."

"It's rather late to begin learning, especially if you are like your mother. She grew up with all these beautiful things round her, but she couldn't state the date or the period of any particular piece and she never learned to dif-

(97)

ferentiate between the good and the worthless—as was proved when it came to judging men."

"She chose a good one."

"She was twenty-eight when she married your father. She had refused a succession of men who, as far as one could tell, had every quality a young woman could desire in a husband —a girl, that is, of her generation. In my day, suitors were screened; if the women had had a wider choice, more of us might have married. You must have had very little desire to know more about your mother—you were three, I believe, when she died and you have only now come to look at the place in which she was born and bred."

Nell had risen and gone to stand on the other side of the fireplace. "I couldn't have come much sooner," she pointed out. "Until my father died and I read the letters and the papers he had kept, I didn't even know that there was a house called Stapling Manor."

Lady Laura was studying her, and Nell met the gaze squarely. She had recovered her poise and was taking in impressions with more clearness than she had done on her arrival. There was not much to be learned, she found, from her great-aunt's face; the only two clues to be picked up as regarded expression was that her eyebrows went up when she was surprised, and down when she was annoyed. Nobody could deny that she was beautiful; add to her looks the tired voice, the see-through look and the frozen manner, and you got, Nell calculated, an impressive total. And it was stimulating, after the first shock, to note the way she threw in insults and then went on without giving you time to throw them back.

"I find it extraordinary," Lady Laura was saying, "that your father took that decision to tell you nothing about your mother's background. I felt sure he would change his mind when the shock of your mother's death had passed, or when he had had more time to get over the strong dislike he felt for me. When did he die?"

"Just over a year ago."

"Now that you're here, how long do you mean to stay?"

"Not long."

"I shall be frank with you. Everything that I have done here—with the exception of making this solar wing into a home for myself—has been done on a business basis. Your mother turned over to me, before she left, the residue of the Stapling capital. It was not a large sum. I could have lived on it, but not in the style in which I wished to live. For that, I wanted far more money, and I may claim to have earned it. I draw the rent from three houses. I receive a certain income from the sale of flowers—they are sent to London. I draw rent from the riding stables, and I arrange performances of *son et lumière* twice a week during the summer. There was a great deal of protest from the people down in the town when I first began to do these things; they considered, rightly, that as I was not the owner, I was not entitled to use the estate for profit. I do not pay any attention to protests. I will concede that I am not the owner, but whether you stay here or go away, I shall continue to take for myself what I have earned by my own enterprise. If you disagree with this, I would like you to tell me so. It will make no difference, but I should like to know your view."

"It's all right with me. I don't want the money, and I don't want to stay here."

"That simplifies the situation. You are very much more intelligent than your mother was. You couldn't very well be less."

"Why say things like that now? She's dead. You didn't like her and she didn't like you, but that's over now—isn't it?"

"Why should the fact that a person is no longer alive be allowed to distort truth?"

"They're not here to answer back, that's why."

"You're doing quite well on your mother's behalf." Lady Laura moved back to her chair. "I advise you to spend a short time here. If you do, I shall try to teach you a little

about these things you see round you—your possessions."
She paused. "Yes, Banks?"

"The trap is at the door, m'lady."

"Thank you. Tell Vincent I shall only be out for half an
hour. Ellen, come along." She stopped on her way to the
door and took from the wall a small, oval frame. "Do you
know who this is?"

"No."

"It is your grandfather. It was done when he was eighteen." She replaced the miniature and spoke with anger—the
first sign of emotion she had shown. "To grow up knowing
nothing of your mother's side of the family . . . I presume
you weren't even told who she was?"

"No."

"Then I see no reason for me to revise my estimate of
your father. Only a cowboy could have—"

"Look, Lady Laura, Great-aunt Laura, Aunt Laura, I
guess we'd better get one thing straight before—"

"I call your father a cowboy because that is what he called
himself. When I understood that he wished to marry your
mother, I felt that as her only relative, I should make some
attempt to find out who or what he was. When I questioned
him, all he said—I give you his own words—was: 'I guess
you can call me a cowboy.' So I did. So I still do. He has
robbed you, and he has robbed me of the chance to meet
while you were still young enough to be formed. You could
have been sent to England, to spend some time with me. You
would probably have disliked me; most people do, but I
have always thought it absurd and wasteful to allow mere
likes or dislikes to operate against the use that one person
can make of another. Your father kept you away, and you
are the loser for his having done so. I could have done a
great deal for you. I could have inculcated taste, and knowledge of beautiful objects. Your mother lacked both. You
resemble her in looks, and you have more intelligence, but

you lack her style. You have a certain poise, but you have nothing of her presence. You have no finesse; since we began to talk, I have been able to follow your thoughts with consummate ease: your attempt to measure me against what you have heard about or against me, your natural resentment at criticism which I feel myself entitled to make, your feeling that Banks is too old to dance attendance on me. Servants like Banks and his son and daughter—who also work for me —are the kind who gain dignity from their surroundings. If I lowered my standards in the least, they would feel cheated. They know what I require, and are proud of their training and ability to serve me. I assist them by adhering rigidly to the rules I have laid down. I shall not, for example, ask you to stay to luncheon, since I consider that a meal prepared for one cannot fill two. Now we shall go. Thank you, I can go down these stairs without assistance. My stick is all I need."

Banks was at the front door, which was open, letting the sunlight illuminate the gloom of the entrance hall. Standing in the shade of a tree was a small governess cart and a stout pony. A groom, an abridged edition of Banks, led the pony forward and held the reins while Banks assisted Lady Laura into the cart and handed her a threadlike whip. Nell took her place beside her, and they proceeded at a leisurely pace along the flower-edged road that led to the lake.

"If you glance back," Lady Laura said, "you will be able to see that I made the conversion of the solar wing without in the least changing the appearance of the Manor. The work was extremely well done, and I was able to fit into the available space all the accommodation I needed for myself and for my servants. We are driving now in the direction of the mausoleum. It's rather hidden away, which is a pity, because it's beautifully proportioned." She stopped the trap and allowed Nell to study the little building with its tiny chapel. "Quite undamaged, as you see. I shall be the last Stapling to be buried there. Beyond this road, there is nothing but the woods, and the heath on which the horses from the riding stable always exercise. I shall turn in the direction of the lake and across it you will be able to see the summerhouse, but I shall avoid driving past it because I am having some trouble with the man who has rented it. I shall get rid of him as soon as I can."

"Is that the archaeologist Mr. Brierley told me about?"

"Yes. His name is Hallam Grant. I understand he came here to revise a book on the subject. He needed a retreat, he said. Do you know anything about archaeology?"

"No."

"Do you know anything about anything?"

Nell smiled. "I guess you can call me a cowboy," she said.

"Didn't you ever leave your father's ranch?"

"Yes, I did. I went away to school, and then we went on trips together. But we didn't talk about furniture and pictures."

"Books?"

"No. There wasn't much time for reading."

"If you had the inclination, you would find the time."

"Maybe. I think I could have read books in a room like the one I met you in, where you couldn't look out and see everything that was going on outside and"—she paused to give a delighted exclamation—"oh, look, that's lovely! All those flowers reflected in the lake."

"Yes, it's lovely."

"And the summerhouse—that's beautiful, too."

"Yes. That saddleback roof was one of the things your grandfather loved." Lady Laura raised the whip and pointed. "On the other side of the wall are the houses I built. They are small, but well-designed. They face the sun, and I planned them for tenants who do not keep servants. I'm afraid there isn't time to go to see the stables. How are you going back to Rivering?"

"My cousin is bringing our car to Mr. Brierley's house."

"Then I may as well leave you here." She reined in the pony and spoke when Nell had alighted. "There is another thing I think you should know. I am negotiating with the members of Rivering Council to buy a small plot of land in the town, to build on it a memorial to the Staplings. The memorial should be up here, of course, but when I am dead, I have no doubt that you will put all this land up for sale, and nobody can foresee what kind of buildings would spring up round the memorial. Everything that I stored in the space that used to be cellars and storehouses, and everything that is in use in the rooms I occupy, will in time be placed in the memorial—or so I hope. I do not see any point in your shipping a few selected pieces across to America when I am dead, leaving an incomplete collection here. The family history is not interesting, but the family possessions are. Very little is left of the grants of land that Henry Tudor gave the first earl of Bosfield, but we have kept other treasures, and when I am dead I hope you will allow them to be put on view. To sell them would be to disperse them. They should be kept together and displayed—furniture, pictures, china, everything. A great deal would have been lost if I had not moved everything over to the solar wing. For this, at least, you have to thank me."

"Thank you."

"I hope you will make no objection to the plan of having a memorial. Perhaps you will send your American friends to see it."

"Maybe I'll even come and see it myself. Did the water from the moat go into the crater?"

"Yes. The water flowed in, but the Americans built a bank to make a lake. They did so much, and so willingly, that I was then and I am still convinced that the bombs which fell were not enemy bombs, but of course I did not say so, and neither did anybody else. Did Cosmo Brierley tell you that

I allow the public into the Manor grounds on certain days of the week?"

"No."

"Well, I do. They pay, naturally. Did he mention the *son et lumière?*"

"Yes."

"Then he will no doubt have told you that when I was planning the performances, I decided to present my own interpretation of the family history. I found no events in the true history dramatic enough to be of any general interest—so I invented some."

"But that's—"

"Quite so. You are going to say that the public would object if they know that what they are watching never in fact took place. Consider their feelings if they came a long way and paid a high price and were then shown nothing of the smallest interest later than the battle of Bosworth. Shakespeare said:

> "For my part, if a lie will do thee grace
> I'll gild it with the happiest terms I have.

"This is the fifth summer the public have flocked to see the *son et lumière,* and there has not yet been any indication that anybody has seen through the gilding."

Nell frowned. "Some of the Staplings must have done something."

"None of the Staplings did anything. The prime object of every earl of Bosfield, from the first down to the last, was to keep himself to himself. It was a tradition, handed down from Richard Stapling, who as a knight was pursued by enemies, robbed of his possessions, hunted, homeless, exiled. He seems to have been left with an exaggerated, one would nowadays say a pathological, desire for security. He rebuilt his home and retreated within its walls, and within its walls successive earls were born, grew up, went out to view the world, found it insecure and returned to the shelter and protection of the Manor. Cosmo Brierley's father produced a history of the family. He will doubtless let you read it. If you do, you will find nothing that would keep a *son et lumière* audience awake."

"Then why give shows?"

"To make money. We have a perfect setting, and thrills can be manufactured."

"Didn't anybody in the family ever do anything?"

"You weren't listening to me; I have just told you that they led long, utterly useless lives. Money was always short; an heiress could usually be found, but her money was invariably used for one purpose only: to keep the Manor in repair. That is why it stood for so long. The daughters of the family married early, or retired to a convent—not latterly, because they couldn't enter unendowed and there was no more money to endow them with. In the last hundred years or so, very few of the women found husbands; men found the combination of title and penury discouraging. And now I will leave you."

"Thank you for—" Nell paused, her hand on the side of the little cart, looking at the upright, motionless figure seated in it.

"For—?" Lady Laura prompted.

"For giving me a lot to think about. When can I see you again?"

"I shall send for you. Where are you staying?"

"At the White Hart."

"When they realize who you are, they will probably ask you to leave. They consider that I have robbed them of their legitimate business—which I have not. Will you please explain to your cousin that I do not receive guests? The only people I invite are those with whom I am transacting business. Goodbye."

A flick of the reins, and the pony was off at a trot. Nell

stayed where she was, deep in thought. The sound of the governess cart died away, and silence fell, broken now and then by a twitter of bird song. In the distance she could see part of the lake; a man was swimming lazily towards the bank near the summerhouse.

She watched him, her eyes narrowed in speculation. An idea had entered her head, but she could not decide whether it was a good one or a bad one. Like her father, she liked to take time to consider any unusual course of action—but like him, she could sometimes give way to an impulse.

She began to walk towards the lake. If it didn't come off, she reflected, then it just didn't; it looked like a good idea from where she stood, but there were other angles. If it worked, it worked.

She reached the summerhouse at the same moment that Hallam Grant, in shirt and linen slacks, came out of it. His eyebrows went up in surprise, but she gave him no time to speak.

"Can I talk to you for a minute?" she asked.

"By all means." He bowed. "Do you fancy the hammock, or would you prefer a chair?"

"A chair. But it won't take long. We don't have to sit down."

"We don't *have* to. We do so," Hallam said, reaching into the summerhouse for a low, cushioned cane chair, "in order to be relaxed and comfortable, for however short a time. May I offer you a drink?"

"No, thanks. Mr. Brierley's waiting for me—at least, my cousin's waiting at his house. I have to get back there. I was on my way when I got this idea."

"You were driving with Lady Laura."

"Yes. She just went home. What I want to ask you . . ."

He held up a hand. "You sit, I'll recline." He settled himself in the hammock and looked at her expectantly. "You wanted to ask me—"

"Will you let me, lend me, I mean rent me your house for a couple of weeks?"

He looked puzzled.

"My house, I don't possess a house. I've got two rooms in London—"

"Your house here. The house you have that's Lady Laura's, only you don't use it much, Mr. Brierley said, because you've fixed this summerhouse up and spend most of the time here." She was speaking, as usual, without haste. "Why I'm asking is, my cousin's kind of old, well not old, but she likes to be warm and comfortable, and down there at the White Hart it's terrible, and the only other hotel is full, and is going to stay full, and I'd like to stay here for a little while, but it seems kind of mean to tell my cousin that, because she wants to go home and I don't think she'd go home without me, and I hate to keep her in that White Hart dump. I wouldn't mind it for myself; I'm used to roughing it because my father said you had to do it young to get to know how to do it if you had to, and you never knew when you'd have to. But my cousin's different. She's never done anything but stay where it's warm and comfortable, so I thought maybe if you wouldn't mind renting us your house . . . well, that's all, I guess."

There was a pause.

"Remarkable," Hallam said at last. "Do you know that you sounded exactly like Lady Laura? The same slow but relentless flow, the—"

"Please. I don't have much time. Could you save the wisecracks until later?"

"I'll try. What makes you suppose that my house is either warm or comfortable?"

"Lady Laura said it was small, and it faced the sun, and she planned it for easy running. There wouldn't be much to keep clean, and—"

"Did you mention this idea to your great-aunt?"

"How do you know she's my great-aunt?"

"You wrote a letter to Cosmo Brierley and sent him into a panic. He came here and I mixed him several very strong drinks. May I do the same for you?"

"I said no thanks. Is it a deal? I know you might want to think it over, but unless you're not comfortable here in the summerhouse, and you do seem to be, then why don't you let me bring my cousin and stay in your house? It would only be for a little while. I'm not going to be here long."

"Why are you staying at all?"

"What did you expect me to do? Make it a day trip?"

"Frankly, yes. I'm only judging by what I should have done if Lady Laura had been my great-aunt. As I'm rather fond of Cosmo, and as he must be in some suspense on this point, I'd like to know whether your decision to stay in Stapling means that you're going to challenge Lady Laura to hand over some of the profits she's been making on your property?"

"No, it doesn't. She can keep the profits. I just told her she could. I just want to stay because . . . is this any of your business?"

"No. You were saying?"

"I can't explain why I want to stay—I just want to, that's all. Maybe because things are different from what I thought they would be. Maybe now that I'm here, I feel I belong, just a little bit. Why should we talk about what I want? Let's talk about how I can."

"Once again I ask—did you mention this idea to Lady Laura?"

"No, I did not. It was kind of beginning to go around in my mind at the end, when she was talking. I'd heard about you from Mr. Brierley, that you liked the summerhouse so much and spend all your time in it, and I figured you wouldn't miss the house for a couple of weeks. Once again I ask: Is it a deal?"

He gave her an unhurried survey, and she found herself with a strong desire to get up and overturn the hammock. She waited with as much patience as she could summon.

"I shall need," he said judicially at last, "time to consider."

"How much time?"

"A few hours."

"What do you have to consider?"

"Whether this plan—letting you occupy the house—would give Lady Laura the opportunity she's looking for, to throw me out. Did she mention her plan of throwing me out?"

"She did say something about getting rid of you."

"What she plans, she performs. There is no clause in my contract saying I can sublet. There is in fact no contract. The only way we can do this is by arranging to make your cousin my cousin, too."

"I don't get it."

"Try," he said encouragingly. "You have come to Stapling to view your property. I do not know you, but guess what, the lady travelling with you turns out to be, what a splendid surprise, whom do you think? No other than my third or perhaps fourth cousin . . . What did you say her name was?"

"I didn't."

"Would you have any objection to being a party to deceit?"

She hesitated, then spoke slowly. " 'For my part, if a lie will do thee grace . . .' "

He smiled. "Let me do the gilding," he advised.

"While you're at it," she said, "would you mind saying it was your idea in the first place? That would make it easier all round."

"*D'accord*. What is my cousin's name?"

"Mrs. Saltry."

"Not cousinly enough. What else?"

"Corinne."

"Corinne. If Corinne will consent to be my cousin, and if she agrees to make a preliminary inspection of the house —this with a view to forestalling any complaints she may make later about its not being warm and comfortable—I am willing to face Lady Laura's onslaught—for onslaught there will assuredly be. She will point out that I have no possible right to sublet, to which I shall reply that there is no possible reason why I may not, on learning that my cousin Corinne was here, suffering untold misery at the White Hart, transfer her to my house and remove myself for a time to this summerhouse."

"Will you be comfortable here?"

"I'm much moved by your concern for me. I was beginning to wonder if you'd overlooked the matter of my comfort. You needn't worry too much; my profession has taught me how to exist in Spartan conditions."

"Is there a bathroom?"

"I said Spartan, not sordid. While the sun shines, I shall bask beneath the trees. When the weather breaks, which it surely will soon, I shall feel less comfortable but more chivalrous."

"Maybe I'll be gone before it rains. Could we settle on a . . . a rent?"

He swung his legs to the ground and sat studying her. Then he rose.

"I'll take the matter up with Cousin Corinne," he said. "Will you give her my love and tell her how happy I shall be to see her again? What is she like?"

"Small and smart. Smart outside and inside, too."

"Married? Widowed? Divorced?"

"All three. Just now she's a widow. She's at Mr. Brierley's house at this minute, waiting for me, so why don't we go there and settle this thing right away? Then Corinne and I could go and eat at the White Hart and pay our bill and come back here and move into the house, if that's all right with you."

"You don't think that's rushing things a little?"

"Is that what you think?"

"I think it's all right with me."

They walked together to the gate and he took a key from his pocket and opened it.

"No trespassers, except on paying days," he explained. "Remind me to give you a key."

"How long," she asked as they walked into the road, "have you lived here?"

"About three months. Three and a half. What did you do between writing to Cosmo and arriving?"

"We stayed in London. I wanted to stay longer, but Corinne had had enough. She's just dying to get back home."

"Where's home?"

"Chenco, Arizona. The ranch is about eight miles away from the town. Or maybe you didn't know I lived on a ranch."

"Cosmo told me. How could your mother ever have expected him to cope single-handed with Lady Laura?"

"How did anybody know, all those years ago, that Lady Laura would do all she has done? She told me I should be grateful to her, and I am."

"She didn't do it for you."

"I know that. You're writing a book, aren't you?"

"Revising one."

"My aunt said you wanted a retreat, but she didn't say from what."

"From people."

"What's wrong with people?"

"Nothing's wrong with some people. But there are others who are the kind who have nothing to do but waste time. As they find it isn't amusing to waste time alone, they look round for somebody to waste time with them."

"That's what my aunt thinks. You could cut off your phone, couldn't you, or lock your door?"

"No use. Nothing is effective except placing yourself

somewhere which is difficult to reach, and not worth reaching."

"When you're through revising and retreating, what will you do?"

"Go back to London."

"Why does Lady Laura want to get rid of you?"

"Because I won a battle. She persisted in rattling past the summerhouse in her chariot, in spite of all my protests. So I emerged from the lake as she was passing. Minus my bathing trunks."

She paused to consider, then gave her opinion. "That wasn't a bad idea."

"It worked. What if Corinne refuses to become my cousin?"

She stopped at the gate of Cosmo's house and spoke with a worried frown. "Look, could we arrange this cousin business without telling—"

"—Cosmo that it's not genuine?"

"He wouldn't like us to do it."

"Certainly he wouldn't be a party to deceit. But how can you stop him from knowing?"

"Can't you think of something?"

The front door opened and Cosmo came out to meet them.

"How did you two meet?" he asked in surprise.

"Miss Berg passed the summerhouse, and I offered her a drink," Hallam said.

Cosmo looked anxiously at Nell. "Did your visit . . . did everything go well?" he asked.

"Beautifully."

They were on the threshold of the drawing room. Mrs. Saltry, her third gin and tonic on a small table by her side, was relaxed and comfortable in Cosmo's best chair.

"How did it go, Nell?" she asked.

"Fine. This is Hallam Grant. My cousin, Mrs. Saltry."

"Saltry? Saltry?" Hallam was frowning. "That isn't a common name. I have a cousin who married a man named

Saltry. I wonder if you've come across her. Her name is Corinne. She . . ."

"Why, I'm called Corinne. How in the world . . ." Mrs. Saltry stopped, staring at Nell, who was making violent signs behind Cosmo's back. "Did you say cousin?"

Hallam had advanced and taken her hands. "This is wonderful!" he exclaimed. "I was in the States in January, and tried to get in touch with you, but they said you weren't . . ."

"That's right." Mrs. Saltry's head was clearing. "I wasn't in Chenco. I was out at the ranch, trying to talk Nell into coming on this trip."

"Do you mean"—Cosmo was looking in bewilderment from one to the other—"do you mean you two are *related?*"

"Cousins, no less," Hallam said warmly. "Corinne, where are you staying now? At the hotel down in Rivering?"

"No. The hotel's full. We're at that place opposite, the White Hart."

"The White Hart?" There was horror in Hallam's voice. "But it's terrible!"

"Yes, I know," Mrs. Saltry agreed. "But there's nowhere else."

"Certainly there is somewhere else," Hallam said with decision. "You and Miss Berg must move at once to my little house—just two doors away from this one. Cosmo, you must persuade her. Tell her I'm hardly ever in the place. It's true, Cousin Corinne. I spend all my time in the summerhouse near the lake. I spent some money fixing it up, and Lady Laura didn't raise a finger in protest—she just raised the rent. She wouldn't, of course, agree to my letting any friends of mine use the house, but a cousin is different. I'm not going to hear of your staying any longer at the White Hart. I'll move my clothes out of the house this afternoon and you can move in this evening and stay as long as you like. Cosmo, persuade her."

"Who wants persuading?" Mrs. Saltry asked. "And don't call Nell Miss Berg; she's a cousin too, if you figure it out.

You know, Hallam, having a base up here would solve everything—Nell could spend all the time she could bear to with her aunt, while I fixed drinks in your house to return Cosmo's wonderful hospitality. He and I . . ." She stopped, her eyes having fallen on a strand of shoelace that had strayed from beneath the sofa. "Maybe, Hallam," she went on thoughtfully, "we'd better just take a look at your house before deciding anything. I mean, suppose it isn't big enough for Nell and me, or something?"

"Come and look at it now."

Hallam led the way with Nell; Mrs. Saltry and Cosmo followed. As they went, Cosmo made plans to bolster up his reputation for wonderful hospitality. He would have to be better prepared for visitors, he decided. He must return what he had borrowed from the Moultons, and then he must get in some little things for Corinne to eat—olives and nuts—in those little dishes people used. And everything must be chilled. Not cold, not iced; chilled was the word she used. And she was Hallam Grant's cousin. How extraordinary that they should meet in his house. Life was indeed full of surprises.

Nell and Mrs. Saltry found the house, when they reached it, to be a replica of the one they had just left—but there was a marked difference in its appearance. Its rooms were almost bare, and clean. The blue-tiled kitchen was tidy, the green-tiled bathroom gleaming. At the end of her inspection, Mrs. Saltry stood in the little drawing room and drew a breath of relief.

"You've made a deal, Hallam," she said. "Is any of this furniture yours?"

"No." It was Cosmo who answered. "It belongs to Lady Laura. She rented the other two houses unfurnished, but put furniture into this one."

"Do you think she's going to make any fuss about Hallam lending us the place?" Mrs. Saltry asked him.

He hesitated. "I really don't see how she can object," he said at last. "If she mentions it to me, I shall tell her that I think it's a very sensible arrangement. Very sensible, indeed."

"We'll be neighbours," she reminded him. "While Nell's catching up on her family history and Hallam's pounding his typewriter, you and I—" She broke off with an exclamation. "Oh, Nell, I haven't told you. Cosmo's given himself a vacation. It's all arranged. Miss Dell—that's his secretary, the one we saw, the one who sees visions or something—she's going to bring up his mail from the office every morning. So we'll see a lot of him. Isn't that fun?"

"I'll take a holiday, too," Hallam said obligingly. "Now if you'll excuse me, I'll clear out some of my things and take them down to the summerhouse, and when I've done that, I'll call on my landlady—if the pennant's flying—to tell her I've lent this house to my cousin."

"And Nell and I have got to get back to the White Hart to eat—and to pack," Mrs. Saltry said. "I'm going to enjoy packing. I can't wait to tell them goodbye."

Hallam went to the door with them, and Cosmo saw them to their car.

"I had three drinks and nothing to eat with them," Mrs. Saltry told Nell as they drove away, "so maybe that's why I can't figure out why I have to have a cousin."

"Did you want to stay at the White Hart?"

"Why did I have to have a cousin before getting out?"

"Because it was the only way Hallam could let us have his house. Lady Laura wouldn't have let him do it any other way."

"Cosmo knew that, so why not include him in the—"

"Because if he knew anything about it, it would make things awkward for him if Lady Laura asked him anything. Anyway, he wouldn't have let us do it."

"Why not?"

"Because he wouldn't be a party to deceit."

"Well, that's a funny way of putting it, but if you mean he couldn't lie about it to Lady Laura, you're right, he couldn't. Did you take a good look at his house, Nell?"

"I didn't have time."

"It was terrible. How could anyone with a heart let a nice old man like him live in a mess like that? Isn't there one woman around here that could help to clean the place up? And look at his office, with that Miss Dell sitting there seeing spooks and not even knowing where to locate anything except her tin of biscuits. He's a sweet old man, Nell, he really is, so gentle, so . . . helpless, so shy and sensitive. He was so glad to have me there to talk with him. I don't believe anybody ever goes to visit him—you could tell by the way he couldn't find anything he was looking for, nice glasses and things, as if he hadn't had to use them for years and years. Maybe when I'm in Hallam's house, I'll help out a little."

"No. He wouldn't like it. And it wouldn't do any good."

"I guess not. I'm sorry I was kind of slow in catching on to being Hallam's cousin. I told you—three drinks on an empty stomach. Where did you meet up with him?"

"He told you—at the summerhouse. Do you suppose he'll really be comfortable there?"

"Who cares? It was him or us. Tell me about Lady Laura."

Nell gave her a brief summary—a purely factual account of the reception, the drive and the dismissal.

"What it sounds like to me," Mrs. Saltry said at the end, "is that she did most of the talking."

"This time, yes. Next time, I'll say more. It's not easy to get a word in—she goes on without stopping, and every so often she throws in an insult and before you've taken it in, she's two paragraphs ahead. You know what I felt like? I felt like a dumb cat sitting outside the hole of a pretty

smart mouse. Every now and again you'd see the flick of
a tail, but before you could put out a claw, it had disappeared."

"I hope she's not going to invite me there and throw
out—"

"No."

"You mean she won't insult me, or won't ask me?"

"She says she never entertains people."

"Well, that's rude, but it's a relief. If we came back and
settled into the house as soon as we've eaten, Nell, we could
catch the *son et lumière* show tonight."

"Is this one of the nights?"

"Yes. Didn't you read that big notice we just passed?"

"No." Nell stopped the car outside the White Hart. "Do
you think it's safe to leave the car here while—"

"It certainly is not safe. I'll get out and take care of the
bill. You drive the car round to the garage, and then
we'll eat."

When Nell had garaged the car and entered the lounge
of the inn, Mrs. Saltry, receipted bill in hand, was leaving
the reception counter. From her expression, and from those
worn by Daise and Betsy, Nell deduced that the operation
had been conducted in an atmosphere less than cordial.

"I paid for our lunch," Mrs. Saltry told Nell on the way
to the dining room. "They made me pay a whole week for
the rooms."

"You didn't think they'd let us off, did you?"

"I told them it was worth it, just to get out."

Nell lifted her head and gave an appreciative sniff. "Can
you smell that, Corinne? A lovely roast."

They took their places at a table indicated by the waitress.
"Did Lady Laura recognize you right away?" Mrs. Saltry
asked.

"Banks did—the old man who let me in. Lady Laura said
I looked like my mother, but I didn't have the same ways."

"That's right, you don't. The big difference, I guess, is the way your mother used to move. Sometimes I'd get a funny feeling she was floating. She had something . . . I can't find the word I want."

"Presence?"

"That's exactly it! How did you hit on that?"

"I'm psychic, like Miss Dell."

CHAPTER

6

The majority of those who came to see the *son et lumière* performances were conveyed in coaches from the neighbouring towns. Spectators were accommodated on rows of hard benches brought up in vans by a contractor from Rivering; they were protected from possible rain showers by a series of awnings mounted on collapsible frames. There was neither warmth nor comfort, the arrangements being made to conform to Lady Laura's edict that every trace of the auditorium was to be removed as soon as the performances were over.

Nell, seated between Mrs. Saltry and Hallam, saw that every bench was full; those who had failed to get seats were herded into groups behind the benches. Beyond the moat, the dark shape of the Manor stood outlined, looking not a façade, but a perfectly-preserved building.

Lights sprang up with dramatic suddenness in a chamber in which, the audience learned, Elfrida, wife of the second earl, was awaiting news of her lover. Horses' hooves sounded in the distance, coming nearer and nearer until they seemed to the spellbound spectators to be clattering over the bridge that spanned the moat. Flickering lights looked like torches waving. Hoarse voices shouted for admittance. The great doors creaked, the tramp of heavy boots echoed. News had arrived, and it was bad news; Lady Elfrida's anguished shriek rose, chilling the blood of the audience and drowning the voice that was recounting the events.

Nell felt herself trembling. At this moment she was prepared to admit that there was a lot to be said for gilding. None of the disillusioning facts she had learned from Hallam could rob her of her sense of participation. It did not matter that members of Mrs. Moulton's pony club had galloped across the stableyard, up and down, up and down, until those responsible for the soundtrack had been satisfied. It did not matter that the Rivering Amateur Dramatic Society had supplied the shrieks and the sound of tramping boots, or that Ernie Lauder's father, an ex-sergeant, had lent his splendid voice for the commentary, or that Mr. and Mrs. Rosenbaum, who owned the café, had filled in the foreign accents. There had lived, once, a Lady Elvira, and she might have had a lover—who could tell? Who, after watching the episode, would be cool enough, fool enough to stand up and challenge its authenticity? The reality was there, across the dark moat; men and women long dead had been resurrected and were speaking across the centuries to present-day men and women and even children (half-price). The fourth earl was there, having arrived with his Castilian bride, and the spectators wept as they followed her slow decline and death in the damp English air. When at last the lights went out, and the outline of the Manor faded and disappeared, and the temporary bulbs above the benches were switched on, the spectators sat silent and motionless; when they moved at last, it was with reluctance, filing out and across the bridge to the waiting coaches with footsteps that dragged.

"Well?" Hallam asked Nell. "For or against?"

"For."

"Good. I was afraid you might prefer history to histrionics. Perhaps before you go away you could persuade Cosmo to come and look at a performance. I haven't been able to. He wants it authentic." He turned to Mrs. Saltry, who was still sitting on the bench, staring at the darkened Manor. "Enjoy it?" he asked her.

"Enjoy?" She dabbed at her eyes with a damp handkerchief. "Who could enjoy it? It was heartbreaking. Why would anybody have wanted to live in those days? How did so many of them live to be old?" She shuddered. "Who wrote the script?"

"Lady Laura."

"Then she ought to go into the play-writing business. When's the next time it's showing?"

"On Thursday. But you shouldn't come again. The second time, the holes begin to show."

"I'm coming, just the same," she said. "I hope I sleep tonight, but I don't think I will. I'll still hear that axe coming down on that block." She stood up. "Let's go. I'm frozen from the feet up. Soon as we get back to the house, I'm going up to bed with a hot water bottle. Nell, will you bring me up a nice cup of hot chocolate done the way I like it?"

They left the benches and walked out to the road that led to the lake. They stopped at the summerhouse to look inside it. It had everything that a camper needed, and a neatness that only an experienced camper could have achieved. There were gas cylinders to give light and heat; a small cooking stove stood on a zinc-topped folding table. A camp bed was made up in a corner.

"What made you decide to work in here, instead of at the house?" Mrs. Saltry asked Hallam.

"The house has neighbours. They're out most of the day, but not all day. Mrs. Moulton's not the friendly type, but her husband is. He dropped in. He kept dropping in."

"So you moved out?"

"Yes."

"Oh, I forgot to ask," Mrs. Saltry said, as they left the summerhouse. "What did Lady Laura say when you told her you'd lent your house to a cousin?"

"She said what I'd expected her to say—breach of contract. That is, breach of no-contract; no gentlemen's agreement workable if one party ungentlemanly. What it boiled down to was one month's notice."

"Notice to quit?" Mrs. Saltry asked in dismay.

"Don't worry," he reassured her. "I won't leave until I want to."

"Will she turn us out?"

"No."

She went up to bed as soon as they reached the house. Nell and Hallam went into the kitchen and Nell, after preparing hot chocolate for Corinne and taking it upstairs to her, took out coffee for herself and Hallam.

"Hot chocolate for me," he said. "A nice cup of Mrs. Saltry's special."

"It's fattening."

"What makes you think I have a weight problem?"

"Your weight."

"This?" He glanced down at his figure. "Pure muscle."

"So you say. You don't go in much for exercise, as far as I can see."

"As far as you can see. I swim, to begin with."

"I saw you. That's not swimming, that's just cruising around keeping cool. Do you go horseback riding?"

"Never."

"Why not? That's good exercise, and there are those riding stables right near you."

"It may be good exercise, but I find it a great nervous strain."

"Nervous? What are you afraid of, for goodness' sake?"

"Horses."

"*Horses?*"

"Yes—you know. Four legs, head and—"

"You should ride them even if you're scared."

"Why? That's an absurd idea, if ever I heard one. I daresay you were born on a horse, and grew up with them. I wasn't. I don't like horses and horses don't like me. I'll stick to skipping. What are you putting in that sandwich?"

"Honey."

"I don't like honey."

"It's not for you, it's for me."

"When you get around to remembering your visitor, I'd like cheese."

"There's no cheese. And there's no more bread."

"I can see a whole half loaf over there."

"That's for breakfast. Besides—"

"Besides what?"

"Bread's fattening."

He put his hands on the table and leaned on them to address her.

"Why don't you come out into the open and call me obese? Why bother about sparing my feelings? My feelings are that I weigh just what a man of my height and width should weigh. I don't say I haven't a spare ounce here and there—all right, make it pounds. Stones, then. I use them to keep out the cold."

"Will you come out riding with me tomorrow morning?"

"Are you in need of exercise?"

"No. But you're the first man I ever met who said he was scared of a horse. I want to see what the horse does to scare you."

He reached over for the bread and began to cut slices, brushing aside her protests.

"Bread," he told her, "comes in time for breakfast. So does milk. So do the newspapers. Is there any ham?"

She handed it to him and he made a thick sandwich for himself and a thin one for her.

"Did you find out," he inquired, "why Lady Laura frightened Cosmo so much?"

"Yes. Dealing with her, you need a thick skin, and his is thin. I haven't got things straightened out yet, but she told me one thing; the money she makes out of this place is hers and nobody else's."

"You agree with that?"

"Yes, I do."

"A pity. It would have been far more exciting if you'd decided to fight for it."

"Why should I fight? If she hadn't done what she's done, this whole place would have been a ruin—no houses, no lake, no restored wing, no nothing. I think she had a lot of courage, fixing things here the way she wanted them. I think she had a hard time in the past."

"The distant past. For the last twenty-five years, she's been living in the utmost comfort, not to say luxury, living as she must always have felt it her right to live. Twenty-five years of warmth should compensate for some of the chilblains she suffered from during her youth."

"Why don't you give her credit for what she's done? She had to have money. Anybody else would have got money by selling off everything, piece by piece."

"Anybody else. Not Lady Laura. What do you think spurred her on to all her money-making enterprises? Her natural energy? She must have been just as energetic as a girl, if not more so. When your mother went away, your great-aunt came into what she considered her own. She became, for the first time, a person in her own right—not the earl's sister, a spinster living with a sister-in-law who didn't want her, and a niece who didn't like her, but Lady Laura, the last Stapling, living in the home of the Staplings. For the first time in her life, she had at her disposal loved objects which up to then she'd only been allowed to see through glass: *Don't Touch*. She was in possession. Nobody could check her. I think she made up her mind then that whether your mother came back or not, she was going to live for the rest of her life as she'd always longed to live."

"Why not? She's been what Cosmo Brierley said he hadn't been—a good trustee. I think she's cheating, showing people all those things we saw tonight, which never happened, but we're cheating, too, pretending Corinne's your cousin. And she's planning to have a memorial, did you know that?"

"No. What does she mean by a memorial?"

"A place in Rivering where all the furniture and pictures and everything can be kept together and put on show when she's dead."

"And you agree with that, too?"

"In a way I do. She said that to sell them would be to disperse them, and together they make a picture of the life of the Staplings." She made more coffee and carried it to the table. "Something I wish I could know is whether my mother would have come back, if she'd lived."

"You mean whether she would have come back in her aunt's lifetime?"

"Yes. Would she? It was six years—three before I was born, and three after I was born. Would six years be long enough to forget all those years she lived here with a sick mother, and with an aunt she hated?"

"Hated is strong."

"Hated is right. How could she live with someone like Lady Laura and not feel something strong, for her or against her? Just seeing her once, listening to her, made an impression on me that . . . I don't think I can explain. If I never saw her again, I'd never forget her. So my mother wouldn't have forgotten what she was like, but maybe she wouldn't have remembered why she'd hated her."

"Judging from what Cosmo told me about her," Hallam said, "your mother was running away from more than her aunt. He knew the Manor well, and he said the conditions of living in it were pretty hard."

"I know. It was crumbling and it was damp and cold and

there was no money and the three of them, my grandmother and my mother and her aunt, were shut up together—how could they have helped getting to hate each other? So I don't know whether she would have come back, but I think my father thought she might, and maybe that made him scared. Why else would he have decided not to tell me anything about her home?"

"Do you wish he had?"

She hesitated for so long that he wondered whether she had heard the question. Then she answered it.

"Yes. I do. I'm not blaming him, don't think that. All I'm saying is that—" She broke off. "Lady Laura blamed him. She said he was wrong. I think so, too, but not for the same reasons that she thinks so. What I feel now, what I realize now, is that this isn't just a place I could come and look at, and then turn and go away again. Part of me belongs here."

"Half of you."

"Yes, half. What there is here is . . . I guess I mean it's a sort of heritage, something I can hand down to my children. Does that make sense?"

"I think so. Who's running your ranch while you're away?"

"Jack Saltry—Corinne's son. He's the person my father wanted to run it, if I didn't want to."

"Do you want to?"

"I never wanted to."

"Why not?"

"Oh, lots of reasons. One was that I never wanted to marry a man and put him in charge—he could never forget I was the owner, the boss. And I never wanted to be the owner and wife and mother, too."

"Why not?"

"Because I didn't, that's why. When my mother died, my father's mother came and helped out, and when I was fifteen, I took over. I liked keeping house, and I liked being with my father on the ranch, but I thought then, and I still think, that they're two separate jobs. Anyway, for me."

"So what do you plan to do? Or don't you know?"

"Yes, I know. Since leaving home, I've had a lot of time to think about it. When we go back, I'm going to talk to Jack and ask him if he'll stay on as manager and half-owner. After that . . ."

"After that?"

"After that, I'll be free."

"To do what?"

"Spread out. See more of the world. Learn more. Come back here and see my great-aunt. Maybe I'll even rent this house when you go away, so I can come here whenever I want to."

"Do you think Lady Laura would like that?"

"She wouldn't care much. All she'll worry about is keeping my hands off the money she's making. What time do we ride tomorrow?"

"We don't. If you want to say it's time I went away, say it more politely."

"Please go home."

"This is my home—temporarily."

"Then will you please go and leave me in your home, so's I can get some sleep? And we're going to ride, whatever you say. I think you're just pretending to be scared."

"Wouldn't it be truer to say you want to watch me making a fool of myself?"

"Maybe. I have to go and see Mr. Brierley first—I want to talk with him. How about eleven o'clock? Will you hire two horses?"

"I shall ask Mrs. Moulton for one horse and one pony. I'd like to keep at least one foot on the ground. Good night. Thank you for the coffee and the sandwiches and the remarks on my overweight. Sleep well."

She slept almost too well; it was almost nine before she opened her eyes. She had a bath and dressed and went quietly downstairs to make some coffee. Opening the front door, she saw bread in a plastic container, and two cartons of milk, and carried them to the kitchen. She thought of taking coffee up to Mrs. Saltry, and decided against it; Corinne had given no sign and probably wanted to sleep late.

After clearing away and making her bed, she walked over to Cosmo's house. Propped opposite his gate was a bicycle of antique design; as Nell came near, the front door opened and Miss Dell came down the path, walking with a jaunty spring.

"Oh, good morning," she called. "I've just taken Mr. Brierley's letters to him. Isn't it a beautiful, beautiful morning?"

"You didn't come up that steep hill, did you?" Nell asked in surprise.

"Oh, no—indeed not." Miss Dell laughed heartily. "Mr. Brierley wouldn't hear of it. He said he would be very angry if I attempted it—which of course I wouldn't, because it would be too strenuous coming *up*, and too dangerous going *down*. No, I came through the grounds of the Manor, on my bicycle. Mr. Brierley gave me a key, and I came in by the far side, by the main entrance, over the bridge and past the lake, but not on the summerhouse side because Mr. Brierley asked me not to. It was very pleasant—the air up here, you know, is very much fresher, very much more invigorating than it is down in Rivering. I enjoyed my ride very much, or I would have if it hadn't been for the risk of meeting . . . I do not care to utter the name. You must forgive me, but I can never bring myself to say it. You will perhaps guess the person I am referring to?"

"Yes. But you can't avoid meeting her if she's driving round the grounds, can you?"

"Ah, *driving*." Miss Dell held up a bony forefinger. "*Driving*. That is what makes it possible. She is never known to walk, and so I can always look out for the governess cart. If I see her in the distance, I shall take what is called evasive action. And now I must go, I'm afraid. I haven't asked your name, but I presume you are a young relative of the Moultons. I have a feeling we have met before. I am Miss Dell, and if you should ever need any dresses made up, or any little alterations done, you will find me in the same building as Mr. Brierley's office. Good morning to you."

Nell watched her out of sight and then turned to find Cosmo coming towards her.

"I didn't come out before," he said, "because it would have made Miss Dell prolong her conversation. Good morning, Nell. Will you come in?"

"Wouldn't it be nicer if you came out? I'd like to talk with you, and it's a lovely morning."

"We shall go to my favourite sunny patch over there; come along."

He led her across the road and they sat on tree stumps in the sunshine.

"First," Cosmo said, "tell me how you got on with Lady Laura."

"I was going to say I liked her, but maybe that isn't the word."

"Admire?"

"Yes, certainly that. How could you ever think that anybody—after they'd seen her—could expect you to keep a rein on her?"

"A stronger man might have made her at least listen to him."

"I don't think so. She said some hard things about me, and she called my father a cowboy—which he was proud to be. She said some hard things about you, too, and about Hallam, and she as good as said she didn't want to see Corinne. And when she wants to see me again, she's going to send out heralds."

"Did she mention money?"

"Yes, she did. I said I didn't want it and she said I couldn't have it, so that made everybody happy. What I wanted to ask you was about furniture. I didn't remember this when I was talking to my aunt, but wasn't there a list among those papers my father didn't show me, a list or a letter from you, about the bomb damage? Not the building—the things inside."

"There should have been a list. I wrote to say that only two or three pieces were irreparably damaged, thanks to the fact that Lady Laura had moved almost everything to the solar wing. I enclosed a complete list of the furniture that remained. I hope your father didn't destroy it."

"No, it's there all right. I remember now—it was pages and pages, and I put it aside and never got back to looking at it properly. Why I'm asking is because it can't all be in the rooms my aunt is living in, and she said she'd kept everything, so where would the rest of the furniture be?"

"It is stored in what were once the cellars. That is one reason why the furniture dealer, Mr. Boutin, comes down regularly. He brings his assistants and they inspect everything that has been stored. He has done this for many years, but Lady Laura has never liked the idea of hiding away so much that was beautiful. Did she mention to you her plan of buying a piece of land in Rivering and—"

"—building a kind of memorial? Yes. She said when she's dead, I shouldn't take anything over to America because everything ought to be kept together. What I'd like to know is why my mother didn't take any of it with her when she went away. Didn't she want anything? Didn't she even want something to remind her?"

He shook his head. "Nothing, Nell. You must try to understand what the atmosphere was during those last weeks. You have only seen Lady Laura once, but you have already felt a little, just a little, of her ruthlessness. You did not oppose her, so you did not discover the lengths to which she will go when opposed, in order to get her own way. Your mother knew only too well. I can say with certainty that if the issue had simply been one of separating your mother from the man she wanted to marry, Lady Laura would have and could have done it. But there was more involved. With your mother out of the way, she knew she would, in a sense, inherit everything that your mother left behind. Has it never occurred to you, since you came here, to ask why your mother endured your aunt, and the life of the Manor, for so long?"

"I was coming to that. Why didn't she get out? Couldn't she have . . . well, gone away, gotten a job?"

"No, she couldn't. To leave the Manor would have meant leaving it for good. She knew that only too well. If she had gone away, Lady Laura would have made it difficult—would have made it impossible for her to return."

"But how could she stop her?"

"By confiscating, by appropriating everything she wanted to make a home for herself. So in the end, your mother went away and left everything. But she knew that although she would never be able to claim what was hers while Lady Laura was alive, she need have no fear that anything would be missing when Lady Laura died. On that point there has never been, there will never be any doubt. Lady Laura will never sell or give away any part of the Stapling possessions."

"How did my father feel, leaving everything?"

"He wanted to . . . his words to me were that he wanted to tidy things up before they left. He was afraid that when your mother had had time to think, she would regret not having taken at least a few of her things to her new home."

Nell sat musing for a time.

"She didn't have much fun, did she?" she commented at last.

"Your mother?"

"Any of them. The house all going to pieces, no money to spend, and not liking each other. That wasn't much of a way to grow up, was it?"

"No, it wasn't. I think the sense that everything had come to an end weighed on them all. Your grandfather died after less than a year of marriage, and your grandmother never reconciled herself to widowhood. She was what used to be called a semi-invalid, which usually meant that the invalid made no effort to get better. She didn't want to live at the Manor, but there was nowhere else for her to go. Lady Laura had her own rooms, but, of course, they had to meet frequently. When your mother left school, she found herself acting as nurse to her mother. No, it wasn't much of a way to grow up, as you remarked."

"Didn't my mother or my father ever try to get anything —later on—that she'd left behind?"

"No. Your father wanted to draw up a legal agreement allowing Lady Laura full use during her lifetime of the Manor and its contents. It wouldn't have made any difference. Legal agreements mean nothing to Lady Laura." He paused. "She has been fortunate, when you come to think of it. Her brother's widow was too ill to oppose her. Your mother was too young. I was too weak. You are too generous."

"There's nothing generous about letting someone have something you don't want—especially when you're going to get it back in the end." She picked up a handful of pine needles and let them drop slowly to the ground. "But I do want just one thing. I'd like her to let me take back something, a kind of personal thing, that belonged to my mother. Something small, that I could take with me by air. Do you think she'll agree?"

"Did you have any special thing in mind?"

"I saw something . . . somehow I felt it would look good in my room back home. Most of the things in that house wouldn't, but this . . ."

"What was it?"

"A little box—about so big. A wooden box, with lovely carving all around it, and the initials *R.S.* in front. That would be Richard Stapling, wouldn't it?"

"Yes. You're speaking of the Bible box."

"Is that what it is?"

"Yes."

"Would you say she'd let me have it?"

"I would say that she would certainly not part with it."

Nell laughed, and got to her feet. "That's what I think, too," she said, "but I'm going to ask her. Then she—"

She stopped. Coming away from Hallam's gate and walking in the direction of Cosmo's was a figure she recognized. She walked into the road. "Good morning, Banks."

He stopped, gave a slight bow and handed her a letter. "From her ladyship, Miss."

Nell drew the single sheet of paper out of the envelope.

I should be glad to see you at luncheon today.
One-thirty. Kindly be punctual.

"Her ladyship," Banks said, with a discreet cough, "said that I needn't wait for an answer."

No answer, Nell thought, meant that it was indeed a royal summons. Or she could conclude, more charitably, that Lady Laura disdained any pretense that she could have engagements which would prevent her from accepting the invitation. She folded the paper and looked up at Banks.

"You knew my mother, didn't you?" she asked.

"Yes, Miss Ellen. When you came to the Manor yesterday, I knew you at once."

"Did you know my father, too?"

"I saw him, Miss, but he wasn't often at the Manor. Her ladyship and he—"

He broke off, and it was a sufficient indication that he had said all he needed to say. He gave another little bow, turned and walked with dignity along the road towards the gateway. She stood watching him, and as she was about to turn away, saw Mrs. Saltry coming out of the house and getting into the hired car. She drew up beside Nell, and called to Cosmo, who was approaching.

"Good morning. Nell, I'm going shopping. Not clothes this time. I woke up this morning and remembered I'm a housewife again—isn't that great? Cosmo, will you please come to lunch?"

"Oh no, no, no," protested Cosmo. "You mustn't go to so much trouble. I lunch every day at the café in the market square, and . . ."

"Not today, you won't. If it keeps nice and sunny like this," Mrs. Saltry said, "we'll eat in the garden."

Nell said that she would be eating at the Manor, and Mrs. Saltry looked at her in surprise. "She's invited you?"

"Yes. That was Banks, the old man who passed the house just as you came out."

"Well, if you're not going to join us, I'll make enough for Cosmo and Hallam and myself. I can't wait to get into the shops and buy homey things like butter and cheese and nice fresh salad. Want to come, Nell?"

"I can't. I'm going over to the stables with Hallam."

"I didn't know he liked riding," Cosmo said in surprise.

"He doesn't. He says he's scared of horses, so I'm going to find what the horses do to scare him."

Mrs. Saltry was about to move away when she was hailed from the front door of the Moultons' house. Down the path came Mr. Moulton, fresh and glowing from his shower, spruce in a well-cut suit and wearing a becoming Panama hat. He radiated goodwill and contentment.

"Wait, oh, please wait, my dear lady! Could you"—he stopped beside the car and removed his hat—"could you by any possible chance be going my way?"

Mrs. Saltry's eyes went from one end of the lane, which merged into the wood, to the other end, which curved down to the town.

"Which other way could I go?" she asked.

"I was using the conventional phrase," Mr. Moulton explained. "Cosmo, will you please present me to these ladies?"

Cosmo performed the introductions, and Mrs. Saltry spoke briskly.

"If you're coming, come," she ordered Mr. Moulton. "I've got a whole lot of shopping to do."

He performed a graceful series of skips to the other side of the car, got in and held his hat aloft in farewell to Cosmo and Nell. Then he settled himself comfortably sideways in order to view his companion. From him emanated a faint, pleasant suggestion of eau de cologne and expensive shaving lotion.

"I can't tell you," he told her, "how delighted I am to have such charming neighbours."

"You're not going to have them long."

"That's a great pity. I do so like American women. We get far, far too few charming women like yourself coming over here, and far, far too many of those dynamic, earnest and if I may say so, boring businessmen."

"Well, just as soon as Nell's through, we're going home."

"Through, may I ask, with what? Don't think me unduly curious; I ask because the answer is of great, I might almost say vital import. Miss Berg is the owner of all that Lady Laura has for so many years been exploiting. Rumour has it that she came here without any previous knowledge of the situation, and so—"

"News gets around fast, doesn't it?"

"My dear Mrs. Saltry, in a place like Rivering, it *flies*. Miss Berg signs the book at the White Hart. The name doesn't ring a bell at first—bells have to ring very loudly indeed before they alert the staff of the White Hart. But when Miss Berg makes inquiries about the Manor, the staff add two and two—the total extent, I assure you, of their mental capacity—and guess that the owner has arrived. I am next in this progression, and I ask myself, why was

Cosmo looking so happy yesterday? Was he happy because he had been entertaining you, or was he happy because there was to be no friction between Miss Berg and Lady Laura? The house I rent is not inside the grounds of the Manor, but it is on Manor ground and I pay rent to Lady Laura. If Miss Berg . . ."

"She's going to leave everything the way it is."

"You take a weight off my mind. And now may I say how glad I was yesterday to know that you were giving Cosmo some of your time? He is a dear fellow, and he has been through some bad times. His marriage was a disaster; one can call it nothing else. She came to Rivering, looked round for a victim, and found one next door—his office was next door to the commercial school she opened. If he'd been living next door to me in those days, I might have been able to save him, but he had rooms in the town, and so he was doomed."

"What was she like?"

"A battleship. Whenever I saw her, I remembered those lines that used to stir me so much when I was nine or ten:

> "Like leviathans afloat
> Lay their bulwarks on the brine

"A leviathan she was. She frightened him, at first, and then she realized that in order to entrap him, she would have to change her tactics. Do you know, I never really believed in women's intuition until I saw the way in which she changed her approach. She was far, far too stupid to have thought it out, so it could only have been intuition that told her that only by making Cosmo sorry for her could she make headway. So she invented a fiancé—I am certain he was invented—who had died, whether in combat or not I can't remember, but certainly conveniently far way, a corner of a foreign field and so on. From that moment, I gave Cosmo up for lost, and lost he was. Now he's free again, and living as he likes to live, but he doesn't get enough society. I'm sorry you're going away so soon. If you stop the car just beyond the next curve, you'll get a very good bird's-eye view of the town. There. Now you can see why it came to be called Rivering—the river curls almost completely round it."

"Does anything ever happen there?"

"Never," Mr. Moulton said with evident satisfaction. "Nothing whatsoever—if you mean, as I imagine you do, anything violent. All the hotheads go away, and we're left with the plodders. The rest of the world seethes and bubbles, and we keep in touch by means of television. I say 'we' because after all these years, I've come to identify myself with the town. The only claim we can make to participation in world events is our unfailing response to appeals. I'm the honorary treasurer of almost everything, and I send off vast sums for crèches, for the poor, the sick, the suffering, the lonely, the aged, the helpless, the hungry and the homeless, refugees and victims of disasters. I'm also chairman of an ambitious little project called the U.C.C.C.C."

"Union of—?"

"—Creed, Country, Colour and Class."

"That seems to cover everything." Mrs. Saltry put the car into gear, and they resumed their journey. "I saw your wife going out this morning—does she always go that early?"

"Always. She usually walks over to the stables, but today she took the car, which is why I'm enjoying this delightful drive with you."

"I saw you running. Do you run every morning?"

"Except Sunday. I don't include Sunday because we're told that we should put aside work on the Sabbath."

"Is running work?"

"Certainly. I am working to keep down my weight—with, as you observe, indifferent success. Do you play bridge?"

"No."

"That's a pity. I have a combined bridge school and club. I should have liked to teach you. Do you know, when I first opened it, about twenty-five years ago, I expected that there would be more men than women joining but the membership is almost exclusively women—sensible, stolid farmers' wives who join in the hope that bridge will prove as relaxing as bingo. I don't want to appear unduly self-congratulatory, but I think I may claim to have risen to the challenge. The curious thing, you see, is that bridge brings out their combative instincts. They come to me tabbies, and turn into tigers. I've never ceased to be thankful for my early training in diplomacy. I think I would have been a great success if I had ever got back to India."

"What were you going to do there?"

"Govern. Now tell me, what does Miss Berg think of Lady Laura?"

"They got on all right."

"I'm glad to hear it. Lady Laura can say things which are rather personal and far from flattering. I don't understand why it's unethical to say things behind a person's back; how much better than having them said to one's face, don't you agree? Do you mind what people say when you can't hear it? I don't. It's usually repeated to one, of course, but it loses its sting at second hand."

"Do you see much of her?"

"Of Lady Laura? I only see her once a month, when I pay my rent."

"Don't you ever get to see her when you're not paying rent?"

"Never. She has inflexible rules, and one of them is that one seal is enough on each agreement. As there could be no contracts, she makes gentleman's agreements. According to the sums involved, one is asked either to lunch or dine— once only. Thereafter, if one calls on her, one is shown into the drawing room and allowed to sit down while one states one's business; then one is shown out. She invites nobody—except those with whom she's contracting business —and she accepts no invitations. Have you any business with her?"

"No."

"Then I deduce that she won't add your name to her visiting list, which is a pity, because although by not meeting you she is depriving herself of a great pleasure, she is also depriving you of the opportunity to see some beautiful pieces of furniture and some lovely paintings. But perhaps you've reached saturation point—haven't you just completed a tour of the Continent?"

"Did you deduce that too?"

"Ah, no. That interesting item was put in train by my friend Charley, of the White Hart, and travelled through a series of tunnels until it reached the energetic and indispensable lady who comes to our house every Saturday to do what is known as the rough; then it came into the open and reached me. Tell me, have you met Cosmo's secretary, Miss Dell?"

"Yes. She was in his office when we went there."

"If she talks about shadows, I hope you won't laugh at her. I have a great respect for her powers."

"I won't laugh. She saw a shadow over me, and it came true. It was Ernie Lauder."

"Ernie Lauder? My dear, *dear* Mrs. Saltry, he didn't, he couldn't have . . ."

"Twice."

"*Twice?* But I must speak to him. I must remonstrate with him. What can he be thinking of?"

"Raising the revenue, I guess."

"But I shall tell him . . . oh, why are you stopping?"

"To let you get out. I've got shopping to do, remember?"

"But these are not the best shops."

"Before going to the best shops, I'm going to park this car where Ernie Lauder won't find it."

Mr. Moulton got out reluctantly and stood bareheaded and beseeching beside the car.

"You wouldn't consider allowing me to accompany you? I could explain the difference between the shops which look best, and the shops which are, in fact, the best. I could—"

"When I shop," Mrs. Saltry told him, "I like to shop by myself."

"Then nothing remains but to thank you a thousand times for giving me a lift and for starting off my day in so pleasant a manner. But I shall only say *au revoir*."

He stood on the pavement with his hat held two feet above his head, stout, pink, cherubic, but oddly dignified. Mrs. Saltry drove away marvelling at the strange biological urges which had drawn him to his angular and dried-up partner. Then she remembered her three husbands, and ceased to marvel.

When Nell arrived with Hallam at the riding stables, she found Mrs. Moulton, jodhpur-clad, grim of face, haranguing a pair of sulky-faced stable boys.

"Swearing," she explained, as she left them and walked up to Nell and Hallam. "Not ordinary swearing—*that* I could allow for. If they were doing it to shock me, they succeeded, but I also succeeded in shocking them. What can I do for you?"

"I telephoned earlier," Hallam said.

"Oh, yes. You want to hire two horses. I take it you're both competent riders?"

"Only one of us is," Hallam said. "Miss Berg."

"You"—Mrs. Moulton fixed Nell with a hard gaze—"are the owner of Stapling Manor?"

"Well"—Nell hesitated—"nobody ever called me that before, but I guess I am—yes."

"I went to see Lady Laura when I heard you were here. I had to ask certain questions, such as why you had come and what you intended to do here. She reassured me."

"What did she reassure you about?" Nell asked mildly.

"The legal aspects of the position. Our contract, for the house and for these stables, is merely a verbal one. My husband and I have always known, of course, that Lady Laura was not the owner of the Manor, but we believed that any undertaking made during her lifetime would be honoured. I was glad to hear her confirm this."

"I'll confirm it too," said Nell.

Mrs. Moulton stared at her through narrowed eyes, decided not to take up the challenge, and turned towards the stables.

"Now we shall see about horses," she said.

The one that was led out for Hallam made him back away.

"No," he said firmly. "It's too big. That's a charger. It could carry Henry the Fifth in full armour."

"This is the quietest horse in the stable," Mrs. Moulton said coldly, "and as steady as a rock. A mere beginner could ride him."

"Don't argue," Nell said to Hallam. "Let's get going."

Like him, she was in shirt and pants. She was astride a horse that was becoming impatient at the delay. Hallam gathered the reins of the gray that Mrs. Moulton was holding, and put a foot into the stirrup. The horse at once began a series of dance movements.

"Tell him to keep still until I'm up, will you?" he asked Mrs. Moulton.

A stablehand came to hold the animal's head. Another put his shoulder against Hallam's haunches and after two powerful shoves, got him into the saddle.

"Fine, you're up. You lead the way," Nell said.

The gray had no desire to lead the way; all its efforts were directed to going backwards into its stable. When Nell set off, it followed in a series of jerks that caused Hallam to slither to and fro in the saddle.

"I don't like them out more than an hour and a half," Mrs. Moulton called after them.

They cut across the wood behind the stable, crossed the bridge and turned on to a wide bridle path that led to open country. Nell put her horse into a canter.

"Hey, whoa!" Hallam called urgently.

She pulled up and turned in her saddle. "What's the matter?"

"You're giving this animal ideas. Whatever yours does, he wants to do."

"Then let him."

"It isn't a case of letting him. It's a case of being unable to stop him."

"Don't stop him. Just let him go. Come on."

She was off, this time at a trot. Following her, Hallam did his best to adjust to the gray's gait, but found himself bouncing helplessly, at times almost unseated. Nell glanced back, reined in her horse and waited for him to come up to her.

"You've got to *trot*, silly. It's easy. You just get the feel of the horse, and next thing, you're with it. Try it again by yourself. I'll watch you."

He dug his heels into the flanks of the gray. Finding this unavailing, he made encouraging clicking sounds. As the animal still stood motionless, he lost his temper.

"Move, blast you," he roared.

The gray moved. It bounded forward, galloped round a tree, left Hallam hanging on a branch, and trotted soberly back to stand beside Nell.

"Get me down," Hallam yelled. "Don't just sit there. Get me down."

At the fury in his tone, Nell did her best to check her mirth. She looped the reins of the gray over her wrist and led both horses to the tree, maneuvering the gray until it was directly below Hallam.

"All you've got to do is lower yourself onto the saddle," she told him. "I won't let him move; I'm holding him."

Cautiously, Hallam felt his way down and regained his seat. His face was scratched and there was blood on his arm.

"Those are the only tricks I know," he stated. "From now on, we go at a nice slow walk."

"Cantering's easier than trotting. And galloping's the easiest of all."

"When you're riding alone, you can do all the cantering and galloping you like. While you're with me, you walk."

"But that's no exercise, for us or the horses."

"Too bad. Now will you move, or this animal of mine will start moving on his own."

She led the way, and for a time both animals acquiesced in the slow pace. Then the gray became restive, and in spite of Hallam's efforts to check it, moved alongside Nell's mount. Later, Hallam was to assert that a plot was hatched between the two animals, but it was some time later, for the next ten minutes were too action-packed to allow time for thought. The gray, without warning, broke into a gallop, and its snort was a clear challenge to Nell's horse to try and race him. Nell's eyes went to Hallam and for a moment there was fear in them, but she saw that he had relinquished the reins and was clinging with both hands to the pommel of the saddle. His eyes were on the trees which were beginning to close in on them. But the gray, avoiding the trees, cut across a dry stream, came out onto open country and settled down to break the Derby record. Hallam slipped steadily down until his arms were clutching the horse's neck. Nell, behind him, could do nothing to help, and decided that the only thing left to do was pray.

It was Hallam who first saw the wall. It was a very low wall, but it was clear to him that the horse would be unable to step over it. His prayers were added to Nell's; he closed his eyes. He felt a sudden braking, and opened his eyes long enough to see the underside of Nell's horse as it rose beautifully to the jump. He followed it across—but the gray did not come with him. When Nell had slipped off her horse and was kneeling beside Hallam to ascertain the extent of his injuries, the gray came to look with mild inquiry over the wall.

"Hallam, are you hurt? Hallam, say something. Are you all right? Is your head . . . why don't you *say* something?"

Hallam sat up. "To hell with horses," he said.

"Are you hurt?"

"Of course I'm hurt. If you're chucked over a wall head first, how can you help being hurt? I hope you're satisfied."

"All you had to do was—"

"I know, I know, I know. Let's not go into it. All I had to do was arrange for my mother to visit a ranch just before giving birth to me." He made himself comfortable with his back against a tree. "If you want to finish your hour and a half, don't let me stop you."

"What are you going to do?"

"Sit here and recover."

"Then I'll sit and watch you." She settled herself close by. "When I tell the boys, they won't believe me."

"Boys?"

"Back home."

"Oh, those. Do you realize that I shall have to pay Mrs. Moulton for having been hurled over a wall and severely injured?"

"I shouldn't have made you come. Why did you?"

"In an attempt to prove to you that a man can be a man standing on two legs, as well as sitting on four. Let it be a lesson to you."

"I'll never forget it. If your mother wasn't on a ranch when you were born, where was she?"

"At the home she went to on her marriage and has never left since—in Somerset. A nice village called Dainley, a nice house called Highmile. I left it when I was twenty—for good, after a nasty scene with my father."

"You seduced a girl and he wanted you to marry her?"

"You've spent too long with cowboys. I left because I wanted to switch from boat-building to archaeology."

"Why?"

"Because."

"Go on. Tell me the rest."

"You collect life histories?"

"I'm starting now. Begin."

"My father, and about four generations before him, are or were boat-builders. Hallam boats—which includes pleasure cruisers, dinghies, launches, speedboats, anything you care to name. The first Hallam set himself up about the beginning of last century, made a fortune and left it to his daughter. She married the foreman, whose name was Grant, and the Grants, father to son, went on building Hallam boats. I always knew I was expected to carry on the tradition; what I didn't anticipate was the earthquake I caused by stating a preference for another profession."

"You wanted to be an archaeologist?"

"Yes. No. I didn't look into the future. All my boyhood was spent learning about the past. I never liked history out of books—the sources always seemed to me shaky; chronicles that had been tampered with, accounts written with a slant, portraits painted to flatter—you could go on and on. I used to read all the books I could find on archaeology. I used to go a long way to meet or to talk to anybody who knew anything of the subject. It always fascinated me, and while I was growing up, I was lucky because there was a lot of change taking place in the archaeologist's world. I used to try to talk to my father about some of it, but got nowhere; he thought archaeology meant grubbing in the ground, finding some old pots, gluing them together and lining them up on a shelf in a museum with neat little labels leaning against them. Even when a team began to unearth some Roman remains not five miles away from our house, he couldn't work up enough interest to walk over and take a look. That was the first chance I got of working with people who knew what they were doing. I was sixteen. And then—"

He paused for so long that she leaned over and prodded him. "And then?"

"And then, in the autumn of that same year, I stayed with some cousins. One of them, the eldest, had a job with a firm of agriculturists and used to fly a little twin-engined job over the experimental fields and make a report. I went up with him, just for the trip. We were flying low and I saw something that puzzled me—odd differences in colouring in a field we'd just flown over. I got my cousin to give it another go, and pointed out what I'd seen, but he didn't see anything unusual. When we landed, I went to a phone and got in touch with the man who'd been in charge of the digging team. He had enough confidence in me to agree to drive out and make a survey—and we found it: the site of a Roman villa. Small, but *there*. Nobody who hasn't done it can tell you what it feels like to learn history from the ground up. My father never understood it and never will. I was born, reared and trained to take over an old-established and successful business, and what was I doing? Throwing it all in his face and talking like a fool about archaeology—and worse—claiming that it was also necessary for me to learn something about architecture, aerial photography, ceramics, mechanics, draughtsmanship and arts and crafts. My unfortunate mother got caught between two cyclones. My father's passion for boats, and building them, was as strong, perhaps even stronger than my passion for trial sections, debris, parallel trenches, deep shafts and local criteria."

There was no basis for compromise. I said goodbye, packed what I felt was lawfully mine, and went to London to study. I worked—God, how I worked! I couldn't get a degree in archaeology in any of the polytechnics or technical colleges, because they're only available in universities. I ended up at Cambridge with a B.A. honours degree—archaeology plus geology. Are you still listening?"

"Yes, go on."

"Chapter Two: I forgot to mention that I've got three brothers, all younger than I am. When I went home on a visit, they seemed interested in what I'd been doing, and I began to write down notes they could look through when they felt like it. I found myself writing not notes, but a short book, easy to read, called *The Approach to Archaeology*. That was all it was—what you'd have to be interested in, what you'd have to know, what you'd have to do if you wanted to make it your profession. It was published, and to everybody's surprise, it sold. It was informative, and I threw in enough about present-day excavation to catch the reader's imagination and keep him reading. So that brought in some money to start me off. At the beginning of this year, the publishers asked me to revise the book. And that's where you came in."

"What do you do when you finish the revising and go back to London?"

"Go to Turkey. Have you ever heard of a place called Kaymakli?"

"Never."

"Or Derinkuyu?"

"Never in my whole life. What are they—tombs?"

"Underground cities. Carved out of soft rock very early in the Christian era. There are seven layers—seven stories, if you like—in the Kaymakli one. It's probable that about fifty thousand people lived down in it. They're not exactly sure who, but probably Christians who used the cities as hide-outs about the middle of the seventh century, when the Arabs invaded Cappadocia. Kaymakli's fantastic—deep wells, airshafts, large rooms and small rooms, drainage channels and rooms used as churches. They had presses for wine and for olives. That's what I mean about evidence, historical evidence. You can *see* this. It's *there*. You don't have to speculate as to how much you can believe—there it is. But when I take you there, when I show you, explain, tell you how much has been uncovered and how much more there is to uncover, how can you be anything but fascinated?"

"Did you say you were going to show me?"

"I did. I can't allow you to go back to your ranch and throw yourself away on horses. Worse, you might marry a man who sits at a desk all day dictating pointless letters to his secretary. Donate your millions to some good cause— say, a hospital for those injured while riding horses. We shan't need millions; I've got all the money a reasonable couple could need. Turn your mind to magic names, magic places. Don't you want to see Pasargadae, for instance?"

"Did you mention Pasargadae before?"

"No. Raise your right hand. Say: 'I, Nell, will marry thee and follow thee to—' "

"—Pasargadae?"

"For a start. Have you anything else, anywhere else, anyone else in view?"

"No."

"Neither have I. That makes two of us, and every successful marriage is made up of two and two only."

"Do you think being thrown over a wall injured your brain?"

"No. My head is quite clear."

"Do you always talk about marrying a girl, the first time you talk to her?"

"This is the very first time—and why? Because I have

always carried—inside me, here—a sketch of exactly what would attract me in a woman. You've got it all. Why should I quibble, or hesitate, or waste time? When I left you last night, I walked round the lake. And round again, and round. I looked at the moon's reflection in the water and tried to compose a poem to you, for you—but the astronauts have put the moon poets out of business. Could Wordsworth say, today: *'The moon doth with delight look round her when the heavens are Bare?'* How could Milton get away with: *'Silent as the moon, when she deserts the night hid in her vacant interlunar cave?'* Silent, with three hundred million of us down here listening to a running commentary? So I went to my camp bed and lay thinking of you. Did you lie thinking of me?"

"No. You said sleep well, so I did."

"I didn't. I didn't want to. I was marvelling at the accuracy with which you'd been built to my specifications. I demanded simplicity, health, humour, beauty, average intelligence and a total freedom from affectation; and there you were. Do you wonder I couldn't sleep?"

"No."

"What I just made to you was not a proposal but a suggestion. A very good suggestion. Off-hand, can you see anything wrong with it?"

"Off-hand, no. But we don't know a single thing, a single important thing about each other."

"We have fifty years in which to find out. I've already given you some details of my past."

"Not your love life. You didn't mention that."

"How much love life do you suppose I had time for, with my head wrapped in wet towels, bent over books? I remember two or three encounters with my landlady's daughter, and there was a girl at Cambridge who had very advanced ideas about free love. Apart from those—oh, I forgot the girl who moved in under the impression I wanted somebody to cook for me—but apart from those, my slate is clean. If I didn't take this opportunity of making my suggestion—my proposition—while you had nobody in view, I would agree that my recent accident had damaged my brain. How many men have asked you to marry them?"

"Four."

"That's a proof that you knew what you didn't want. Was there an archaeologist among them?"

"No. Before you make proposals, propositions, suggestions, maybe you ought to find out whether a girl would make a suitable wife for an archaeologist."

"Archaeologists are built like other men; where's the problem?"

"Their wives have to know something about what they're digging for, don't they?"

"I shall teach you."

"Why can't you be serious?"

"Do you seriously think I'm not?"

Their eyes met. The silence lengthened.

"Do you?" he asked again.

"Maybe not. But you're . . . you're going too fast."

"What do we have to wait for? We're not children, are we? At twenty-three and thirty-one, aren't we adult enough to know what we want? If you'd earned your millions, I might have been worried, because I'm old-fashioned and I like to think of man as the wage-earner—but you didn't earn them, you merely inherited them, and I've told you what you can do with them." He rose, drew her to her feet and, still holding her hands, laid his lips on hers. "That wasn't a kiss," he said, releasing her. "It was a seal. A seal on a bond."

"A gentleman's agreement?"

"Exactly."

They stayed out the full hour and a half, and they walked back to the stables, leading their horses. As they came in sight of the buildings, Hallam remembered his fall, and turned to Nell.

"How do I explain these scratches on my face?" he asked.

"Don't bother to explain," she said. "They'll never believe it was the horse."

CHAPTER

7

The drawing room, on Nell's second visit to the Manor, had not lost its look of gloom. Nor was there much change in Lady Laura's appearance, except in regard to colour; her dress and hat were of pale mauve, the hat being covered with a mass of tiny mauve feathers. She was standing by the fireplace when Nell entered, and came forward to greet her and indicate a chair.

"Sit there," she instructed. "I shall take this high-backed chair; I can't be comfortable in any other kind. I'm glad to find that you're punctual. It was not one of your mother's virtues. You see something of Mr. Grant, do you not?"

"Yes. He—"

"Has he told you that I object most strongly to his handing over to you and your cousin—his cousin—the house he rents from me?"

"He did it because—"

"It was extremely high-handed, and I am extremely angry. He should have come to me for permission before offering it to you."

"—because Mrs. Saltry wasn't comfortable at the White Hart. Now she's happy because—"

"I am not interested in Mrs. Saltry."

"—she can housekeep. She likes to play at it."

"Play at housekeeping?"

"Yes. If she had to fix three meals every day, she couldn't do it, but she can fuss up salads and egg dishes. I don't think Hallam should be turned out just because he got us out of that awful inn."

"Hallam? Are you on such familiar terms?"

"No. We just call each other Nell and Hallam."

"You went riding together, I'm told."

"Not far. He fell off."

"But you were out the full hour and a half."

"That's right. You've got an information bureau, or something?" Nell inquired with genuine interest.

"I make it my business to know what is going on round me. I make a tour of the estate every day, and I go past the stables. I have no wish to interfere with anything you choose to do here, but I hope you will remember that you are my great-niece. How can you spend your time sitting about under trees with a man you've known barely two days? Especially that man. You may have inherited your mother's gullibility. Her attraction was her title; yours is your money."

Nell gave her a long, astonished stare. "What makes you think that way?" she asked in amazement. "You're so nice to look at, so clever at managing things, you've got everything the way you want it, you've got lovely things to look at and live with, and you said what's true: that you could teach me a whole lot. But there are things I could teach you, too, like—for instance—what it is about a girl that matters to a man, an honest man, more than titles or money. Wasn't my mother beautiful? Didn't you say we all were, all the Stapling women? If my father had cared about her title, wouldn't he have told people about it at home? He

didn't, because he wanted her to be just plain Mrs. Matthew
Berg. I know you and my mother didn't get along, and there
were reasons why you didn't, but they don't apply between
you and me. I like you. At least, I'd like you if you didn't
keep saying insulting things about my mother. I—"

"Have you finished?"

"Not by miles. I like you and I admire you and I'm glad
you've given me this chance of seeing how my ancestors
lived. I couldn't live this way, but I'm glad you do, because
it's part of you and you're part of it. So why can't you
forget you didn't like my mother, and try to get around
the other side of her and take a look at me? I'm staying in
Hallam's house for only one reason: to get to know more
about you, to see a little more of you before going back to
where I belong. I'm not what you said—gullible—and
neither was my mother, but I'm going to sit under a lot
more trees with Hallam because we like each other and we
haven't much time to find out how much more there is in
it. You can't call him a cowboy, because he climbs up one
side of a horse and falls over the other. He isn't after my
money; he's told me what to do with it. So there's the
picture: me, you, Hallam—and his house that he rents from
you. Please don't turn him out of it. Now I've finished,
and thank you for listening, but maybe you don't feel any
more friendly than when I started."

"You have been very frank."

"No, I have not. The trouble with you, Aunt Laura, is
that you scare people into doing things they're ashamed of.
Like Cosmo Brierley, ashamed because he couldn't make
you listen to him. If you'd listened, all you would have
heard was that he thought my mother, or my father, should
be told—by you—what you were doing here. That's all.
And you didn't scare Hallam, but he knew he couldn't hand
his house over to two strangers, and so when I asked him
to let us have it—"

"You asked him?"

"Naturally. The only way was for him to let his cousin have it, but Corinne isn't."

"Corinne?"

"Mrs. Saltry."

"She isn't what?"

"His cousin. Only my cousin."

"So he lied?"

"Of course he lied. The idea was a good one. The arrangement was sensible and convenient. It made me happy, Corinne happy to be comfortable, Hallam happy to oblige, and Cosmo Brierley happy to take a vacation and see his new neighbours. Four people, acting reasonably—against one acting unreasonably."

"Do you realize that you're being unforgivably impertinent?"

"Only if you look at it that way. It seems to me that you can be friends with me—or you can do what Hallam's horse did this morning: get mean and stay on the other side of the wall."

"Be friends? When you have just told me that there has been a conspiracy of lies—"

"I wouldn't have told you if you hadn't called me frank, giving credit where it wasn't due. Or maybe I just told you because if you're going to turn Hallam out of the house, it didn't matter anyway. Only look at you: beautiful, elegant and as far as appearances go, right up to the present-day minute—but what's the use of all that if your outlook doesn't keep pace? My grandmother—not this one, the other one—always told me that no matter how long she lived, she wanted to go on changing her views. She said that if you're eighty and thinking the same way you did when you were fifty, you've been dead for thirty years without knowing it. I'm twenty-three—and I was born three years after my mother was married. That adds up to twenty-six years—which is too long for you to go on remembering that you didn't like her."

"Didn't you say, some time ago, that you had nothing more to say?"

"I guess I got worked up. Wound up. I'm sorry if you're angry, but what I'd like to do now, if it's all right with you, is to stop talking and start looking. If there's time before we have to eat, couldn't you show me around?"

Lady Laura said nothing. She merely rose and led the way to the door from which she had entered on Nell's first visit. It led into a corridor from which opened two large bedrooms and two bathrooms. The bedroom not in use was simply furnished, and had little more in it than two matching beds with heavily-carved canopies. Lady Laura's room had a large double chest in one corner and a beautiful drop-front desk in another. The bed was regally draped, an imposing sight with red velvet hangings and a magnificent matching bedspread. At its foot was a long daybed covered with beautifully worked tapestry cushions.

"All the needlework in the house was done by Stapling ladies," Lady Laura told her. "Including your mother and myself. My eyes are not as good as they were, but I can still embroider. Were you taught to embroider?"

"No."

Nell spoke absently, her mind being full of the thought that these rooms needed only a rope across them to complete the resemblance to the disused royal apartments through which she had trailed in the wake of official guides.

Lady Laura smiled faintly. "You are thinking, no doubt, that I could live in a simpler style. I could, of course, but I don't choose to. Why should I send away my servants, put my furniture in storage and retire to a little box or chicken coop or hotel? The fashion, nowadays, is to reduce one's life to the drab general level. One may be rich, but one must not be grand. People spend fortunes on travelling comfortably, but are ashamed to be seen living comfortably. If there are servants, they must be treated like one of the family; the daily help must be introduced and shaken hands with. I don't know your views on the subject."

"I couldn't live . . . I mean, I think everything in these rooms is beautiful, but . . . not for living with. One or two pieces, maybe, but not all around me."

"You find them overwhelming?"

"Not overwhelming. Kind of heavy. I want big soft chairs to curl up on, floors I don't have to polish, great big windows and built-in cupboards. That's for me—but not for you. You go with this background. You're part of it. The word is stately, and that's what you are. I couldn't see you in a box or a chicken coop. This is you, and I'm glad I've seen you, and seen the way you live, because for the first time, I can really see my mother and understand how she lived."

"Don't make the mistake of thinking that she was as comfortable as I have made myself. If you want to recreate the past, you will have to take certain facts into consideration —notably, the lack of money. To keep up the Manor in those days was a very different thing from keeping up a few rooms, as I do now. There was no heating, except for open fireplaces. There were servants, but not enough. All the un-married daughters of the family, before me, had had allow-ances, however inadequate. I had no money at all; my father, and later my brother, pointed out with perfect truth that they had none to give. Your mother turned over to me, when she went away, what remained; I took it because I felt that some of it was rightfully mine. Then I turned my attention to making this place pay. It does pay. It doesn't pay much more than I need to live here with three servants, but I am comfortable, I am independent, and I am living, at last, as I would have liked to see my father and my brother living. I am the last, but, thank God, I have succeeded in snatching something from the past. And now shall we go back to the drawing room?"

Settled once more in the high-backed chair, she let her

eyes rest speculatively on Nell. "You've talked to Cosmo since meeting me?"

"Yes."

"He wanted to marry your mother—I suppose you've sensed that?"

"I know he must have been very fond of her."

"He was in love with her, but he never told her so. That is, he never put it into words. I suppose he saw she wouldn't have had him, but there's a great deal of the doormat in him; he invites being trodden on. Did he show you the full extent of the property?"

"No, but when I was out this morning, horseback riding, I saw—"

"—the original domain. Do you know what a domain means?"

"It's the land owned by the Manor."

"Yes. It was divided between the lord of the Manor and his tenants, who were called vileins and who were bound to work for him for a certain number of days in the week or the year. Vileins had certain rights in their holdings which were recognized by law. Manorial courts dealt with any business concerning the manorial holding."

"Is that what Sir Richard Stapling was—lord of the Manor?"

"Yes. Before the end of the Middle Ages, the system was beginning to decay. As is the case today, the vileins wanted to get off the land and move to the cities. If they resided in a town for a year and a day, they were made freemen. One of the things destroyed by the bombs was the record of the number of vileins who left Stapling Manor. There were also records of the manorial courts, but not many and not in good condition."

"Is there a portrait of Sir Richard Stapling?"

"In the dining room; you'll see it when we go in. Have you decided when you are going away?"

"No."

"While you're here, I think you should come to see me—but I shall not invite you. You have only to look at the pennant, to see if it is flying; if it is, I am here and I shall be glad to see you and tell you anything you want to know."

"Thank you."

"I caught a glimpse, this morning, of Cosmo's so-called secretary. What was she doing up here?"

"She's going to bring his letters while he's away from the office."

"She claims to see visions. I think Cosmo is very unwise to employ her."

"He said something about you; do you want to hear?"

"Not in the least."

"Then I'll tell you. He said you had been a good—"

"—custodian? So I have. He isn't really the authority on our family that he claims to be, my dear Ellen. He may have thought it his duty to go round the Manor like an auctioneer's clerk, listing its contents, but it was nothing but a waste of time; I know more about the Manor and its contents than he ever could. What he really expected, of course, was that your mother would write to him sooner or later and ask him to try and send her some of the pieces she had left behind. I should not have given them up. On the other hand, I should never have agreed to sell them or to give them away."

"Didn't you *ever* get on, Aunt Laura, you and my mother?"

"Never. Perhaps there was too little difference in our ages—I was only fifteen years older than she was; too old to be a sister, too young to be an aunt. I made no secret, after my brother died, of my dissatisfaction that he had left me nothing—I mean that he had not named specific pieces of furniture, or certain pictures, which were to be mine. I was only fifteen when he died, and I daresay he thought that I would marry—but as I told you, a girl with a title and absolutely nothing to go with it wasn't likely to attract many men. I didn't like my brother's widow; I thought and still think that if she had made an effort, if she had given up drooping on sofas, if she had made some attempt to pull herself together, she could have been healthy and useful, and the atmosphere would have been considerably lightened. But she preferred to droop. And the tradition of repairing the Manor continued—a constant, unending drain on the money that remained. Do you know how I grew up? With a series of governesses, with only my brother as companion, ten years older than myself. A home full of treasures, but no people invited to stay, no entertaining, no gaiety of the kind young girls expect. I had no dowry. I was lonely and bored—what today would be called frustrated. Your mother and I might have found some common ground if she had felt the same pride in the family as I did but she refused to see herself as the last of a long and honourable line; she thought that we had held on too long to something which should have been allowed to disintegrate. She stayed at the Manor because she was afraid that if she went away, I would lay claim to what was hers—and she was right. She had possessiveness without pride. But she went in the end—shook off her birth and her background and went away leaving them lying like discarded clothing. She took nothing with her, and swore never to return while I was alive. That is why I regard these things as mine, and this as my home. The things round me are my husband, my children, my friends. I have never parted with them and I never will. Have you anything you wish to ask me before I order luncheon?"

"Yes. Before I go away, would you give me something, a small thing, that belonged to my mother?"

"No, I will not."

"Would you let me buy it?"

"No. I am old. You won't have long to wait. What, particularly, did you have in mind?"

"That little wooden box."

"The Bible box?"

"Yes."

"You cannot have it, but I applaud your taste. It is beautiful. It belonged to Richard Stapling. You can still see his initials"—she rose, lifted the box and carried it to Nell—"beautifully interlaced with the carving at the front. Whenever I look at it, or at the cellaret in the dining room, or the little envelope table over there—all small enough to have been packed without trouble—I feel incapable of understanding how your mother could have left them behind. They are among my most treasured possessions. I have had many offers from people who want to buy that Bible box, but I won't part with it—or with anything else. And now will you please pull that bell-rope? I should have explained that I don't offer anything to drink before luncheon or dinner. I detest the modern short-drink habit. Do you drink much?"

"No, not much."

"Do you take drugs?"

"No."

"Have you had love affaffirs?"

"In the way I think you mean, no. Not so far."

"You seem singularly free from the weaknesses of your generation."

Nell met the hard gaze, and smiled. "All that healthy ranch air," she explained.

Banks came in to say that luncheon was served, and withdrew. Lady Laura rose and Nell handed her the walking stick.

"Have you a husband in view?" Lady Laura asked.

"I didn't have when I came here. When you were a girl, did you have a sketch in your mind of the kind of man you'd like to marry?"

"No."

"It might have been a good idea. Then, when you met someone, you'd know at once whether it was a perfect likeness or not."

"Was that another of your Berg grandmother's theories?"

"No. Hallam's."

Lady Laura, who had been walking slowly towards the dining room door, held open by Banks, paused before they came within earshot, and turned to Nell.

"I hope you're not going to make your mother's mistake of rushing headlong into marriage," she said coldly.

"Only hers wasn't a mistake."

Lady Laura walked on in silence. They entered the dining room, which looked to Nell to be a mile in length. At the beautiful refectory table, two places were laid—Lady Laura's at the head, Nell's at her right. A wide piece of Chinese embroidery ran down the empty space, and on it at intervals stood four silver bowls filled with rosebuds. Portraits hung on the walls, silver and glass twinkled from the heavy sideboards. Nell took her place, opened a table napkin two feet square and directed her attention to the portraits.

"Who?" she asked.

"Your great-grandfather, his father, his grandfather. There was no portrait of your grandfather—nothing except the miniature in the oval frame which I showed you in the drawing room. Your mother was painted when she was eighteen; your father took the portrait with him when they went away."

"It was in his room. It's still there."

"The portrait at the end—the last in the row—is not a good one. It shows your grandmother with your mother, but the likenesses are not well caught. Will you take white wine with your fish?"

"Please."

Assisting Banks was his daughter, neat in black. The serving dishes were of silver, the wine glasses delicate, the knives and forks heavy, the family crest so worn as to be scarcely discernible. The food was as good as Nell had expected it to be, but there was even less of it than she had anticipated. So far, she had been given the thinnest slice of melon that ever stood alone; it had been followed by creamy, delicious sole which she did her best to divide into four mouthfuls, but swallowed in three. Now they were waiting—for what? Meat, she hoped, with potatoes and a green salad.

There was no meat. Plates of exquisite colouring and design were placed before them. Grapes were offered, finger bowls set in place. Nell, struggling to cut a branch of the grapes with silver scissors of great beauty and antiquity but no cutting edge, told herself that there was no longer any need to ask why her mother had left home.

"I do not take coffee," Lady Laura said, rising from the table, "but I have no doubt that you do. Banks will serve it in the drawing room."

Little was said until Banks had placed the small silver tray at Nell's elbow, and withdrawn. Then Lady Laura spoke in a tone that was slightly more businesslike than her normal, languid voice.

"Have you thought over the scheme I outlined to you yesterday?" she asked. "I mean about placing the Stapling possessions in a memorial hall?"

"If you mean do I have anything to say against it, then no, I haven't. The only thing is that I'm sorry it won't be on Stapling ground."

"I have told you why. The remaining walls of the Manor will crumble, an eccentric antiquarian will perhaps make an offer for the mausoleum, the land will be sold, the moat and the lake will be filled in and a forest of ugly little houses will spread over this hill. Neither you nor I need concern ourselves with that; I shall be dead and you will be many thousands of miles away with the husband you are looking for—and will undoubtedly find."

"I might find him nearer than that."

"I don't think Hallam Grant will attract you sufficiently to keep you here. You will go back to America, and like your mother, you will be content to use Cosmo Brierley as your sole link with this place." She paused. "As you have no objection to the idea of a memorial hall, we can discuss the financial aspect."

"What financial aspect?"

"The choosing of a site in the town, the plan of the hall, its eventual arrangement—these details you may safely leave to me. But I cannot afford to carry out the plan. I am looking to you to provide the means."

"You mean you want me to pay for it?"

"Precisely. Did you imagine that I could, or would?"

"I just thought that you'd had this idea, and wanted to know what I thought before going ahead with it."

"You will be paying—if it means anything to you—for a lasting memorial to your ancestors. I shall draw up an estimate and hand it to you, or to Cosmo Brierley; he will examine it and give you his opinion, which may interest you but which will not interest me. There will be a number of details to discuss; I hope you will be able to stay here until we've arranged all there is to be arranged."

"How long?"

"Not more than a week or two. Can you arrange to stay for two more weeks?"

"Yes. Corinne won't like it, but . . . yes."

"Then that's settled."

"You said something—two things," Nell said, "which I didn't understand. First you said you didn't entertain people, and then you said you'd had offers from people who wanted to buy things. How do people know about them?"

"A sensible question. Twice a month, I go up to London. Whatever other business I have, I always pay a visit to Mr. Boutin, of Boutin and Bale. They are antique dealers, known by collectors all over the world. Mr. Boutin keeps me in touch with present-day values of furniture. When he has a customer who is looking for something special to buy, he sometimes telephones to ask if he may send them here to look at my oldest pieces. He only sends foreigners, or

Americans or South Americans—people in England for a short visit, who have no time to go round museums or collections. Have you had all the coffee you want?"

"Yes, thank you."

"Then I won't stand on ceremony. I always like a rest after luncheon, reading or sewing in my room."

Nell rose. "If there's no ceremony, I'll let myself out without having Banks looking to see if I really go. Thank you for asking me. Did you mean that about coming to see you whenever the flag's flying?"

"Certainly."

Nell came two steps nearer. After a perceptible pause, Lady Laura reluctantly offered a cheek. Nell kissed it gently. "Goodbye, Great-aunt Laura."

She let herself out of the great double doors, closed them behind her and walked in the direction of the lake. The summerhouse was closed, a fact which surprised and disappointed her. She used the key Hallam had given her to open the iron gate and then went into his house and walked straight to the kitchen. When she had closed the door of the refrigerator and turned, a cold leg of chicken in her hand, she found Hallam getting out a loaf of bread and preparing to make sandwiches.

"Where did you come from?" she asked in surprise.

"I was waiting in the drawing room, like a visitor. When I saw you streak past into the kitchen, I knew what was the matter. It can't be as bad for you as it was for me—a man needs more filling. She gave me three shrimps on a bed of lettuce, one lamb cutlet with delicious potatoes the size of marbles, and one peach. Here you are. There's cheese in that one. Tomato coming up."

"When did you eat with my aunt?"

"Every incoming tenant gets a meal. Eating her salt takes the place of a formal contract. Thereafter, you don't get invited. You may call, you may converse, but you don't eat."

"Where's Corinne?"

"Upstairs, taking a siesta. When you've eaten all you want, I thought we'd go to the summerhouse. When you've had time for digestion, we'll swim. I've brought you Cosmo's father's history of your family. Dull, I fear."

"But true."

"Absolutely authentic, so Cosmo assured me. How did you get on with your aunt this time?"

"I told her Corinne wasn't your cousin. I thought she . . . what's so funny?"

"You." Hallam controlled his mirth. "Go on—tell me."

"I told you. I told her. I said a lot, but you can't tell whether she's taking it in or not. She wants me to pay for that memorial she's going to build to the Staplings."

"You sound surprised. Did you think—"

"—she could, or would? Yes, I did. You know something? She goes around with her eyes and ears wide open. She knows all about sitting under trees and staying out for an hour and a half."

"That doesn't surprise me."

"It surprises me. It's snooping."

"There are kinder terms for it. It makes her more human, doesn't it?"

"Maybe. I told her I couldn't live the way she does, all shut up with all those things. How did my mother stand it? When she got to the ranch, she must have thought she'd gone to live in a fish tank. What did Corinne make for lunch?"

"Chicken salad. Very good. Cosmo thought so, too. She's cosseting him, and he's enjoying it."

Cosmo was waiting for them when they came out of the lake. He had stopped at the house, he told them, and hearing no sounds, had come on to the summerhouse.

"Then Nell can make us some nice tea," Hallam said.

Nell made it and carried it out to the table that the men had put up. She handed Cosmo his cup and gave him a short account of her visit to Lady Laura.

"She's going to draw up an estimate of the cost of the memorial," she ended, "and she'll show it to me, and I'll show it to you, and after that, all I have to do is pay for it."

"It doesn't only mean paying for the land and the building," Cosmo pointed out. "There'll be the upkeep."

"Which includes a caretaker," Hallam said. "That would be a good job for Miss Dell. She could show people round, and nobody would mind much whether she got the history straight or crooked."

"I asked for the Bible box," Nell told them. "I didn't get it. No sale, and no hand-outs. Is it true," she asked Cosmo, "that people come down from London just to see her furniture?"

"Yes. They're sent by the furniture expert, Mr. Boutin. I'm sorry about the Bible box, Nell. She shouldn't have let you go back without something of your mother's."

"Who says she's going back?" Hallam asked lazily from the hammock.

Cosmo was so startled that his tea spilled over into his saucer. "I don't understand. Has Nell changed her plans?"

"No, I haven't," Nell said.

"Then what did Hallam mean?"

"Only Hallam knows."

"I've advised her to take up archaeology," Hallam explained. "With myself as guide, teacher and husband. I frightened her by mentioning far-off places, but she could make a start in this country by touring the lost villages they're discovering. Only twenty-three in Suffolk so far, but one of my brothers has joined a team there, so we can expect the total to rise. Extraordinary to think of him going the way I went. He wrote me several pages about villages that were built over Norman manor houses. In centuries to come, they'll be writing about the village that was built over Stapling Manor. What more can a girl ask than a good man engaged in the most fascinating of all pursuits?"

"Nothing," Nell said. "But there are plenty of good men,

and more than one fascinating pursuit. . . . There's more tea if anybody wants it."

"No, thank you." Cosmo was still looking shaken. "Hallam's joking, of course?"

"He says he's serious."

"Isn't it"—Cosmo addressed the question to Hallam—"a little, how shall I put it, precipitate?"

"If you mean I'm acting on impulse," Hallam said, "you never made a bigger mistake. My declaration was made at the end of a long, lonely journey. I turned a corner, and there was Nell. Do I walk on, leaving her to those other good men she claims to know?"

"You pause, surely?" Cosmo suggested.

"For what?"

"To give her time to . . . to . . ."

"To argue? If she doesn't know by this time whether she wants me or not, there's something wrong with her reactions. Have you any doubts as to my making her a good husband?"

"As far as one can tell—" Cosmo began.

"That's just what I told Nell. We've got fifty years ahead of us to fill in details. I'm relying on you to back me up."

Cosmo seemed overcome. He fell into a reverie, and they left him in peace. When at last he roused himself, he looked at his watch.

"Will you forgive me if I leave you?" he asked. "I told Mrs. Saltry that I would drive down to the town with her after tea."

They forgave him, and he left them, and Hallam gazed after him thoughtfully.

"Would you say he was unduly impressed by Corinne?" he asked Nell.

"Not unduly; just impressed. She's good at impressing old men. She makes them think of womanly charm, and sympathy, and experience blended with . . . work it out for yourself."

He made no reply. He was swinging gently, balancing his cup and saucer on his stomach. She watched him in silence, and then her eyes went to the quiet lake. She felt restless and uneasy; she was accustomed to knowing her own mind, but now her mind was anything but clear. There was too much all at once, she thought—there were too many new ideas, new angles, new relationships.

He lifted the cup and saucer, finished his tea and swung his legs to the ground.

"Cold?" he asked.

She drew her towel robe closer round her, but shook her head. "No."

"Tired?"

"No. Confused, I guess."

"Then you want a change. I'll get my car out and drive you somewhere."

"Where?"

"What does it matter? Go home and dress. I'll come and pick you up in twenty minutes."

She went away without answering, and he watched her go, his heart turning in pity. Her cousin wanted to get her back to America. Her aunt wanted her money. He wanted her—not her money—herself. He wanted her to trust him but there was no time to build up trust. There was not enough time to build up in her the certainty he felt within himself. But he would do what he could in the time the fates had allotted to him.

They drove without purpose, choosing quiet lanes that led away from the traffic on the main roads. They stopped to drink beer in a thatched-roof inn called the King's Bounty, and then drove on through the darkness and stopped within sight of Rivering, on the far side of the bridge that led into the town. They could see the lights of the cars, lighted houses, the glow that indicated the market square, but there was no sound near them but the gentle lapping of the river against its banks.

"There's a song," he said, after a long silence. "Something like this:

> "Keep close beside me through the long dark night,
> Stay close beside me till we reach the light.

"Ever heard it?"

"No. Do you always sing out of tune?"

"Only when I'm moved, as now. I enjoy my singing."

"Do you know when other people are singing out of tune?"

"You can't tell, these days; everything's off key. I used to sing solos in my school choir."

"We didn't have a school choir. We had a school orchestra and they gave me something called a triangle to play, and I thought it was tame, so I quit. That was the first time I ever remember Corinne coming to see me at school. She tried to make me go back to the triangle. All the girls thought she was pretty, but I didn't—not then. I thought so when I got to be older. Do you think she's pretty?"

"No. She's good-looking in a trim sort of way."

"But her eyelashes—she had the longest eyelashes of any girl in Chenco, when she was young. Men couldn't resist her eyelashes. One blink, and they were goners."

"What was the use of blinking in the dark, if it was dark? She couldn't have—"

He stopped. The next few moments were confused. A pair of arms went round his neck. A heady mixture of powder, cream and fresh young body rose to his nostrils. A cheek was pressed against his own and a voice spoke softly.

"Keep still. Can you feel anything?"

He would not have cared to state what he was feeling. Against his cheek there brushed, once, twice and again, her eyelashes.

"Are you there, Hallam Grant?" she whispered.

"I think so."

The soft brushing swept his cheek again.

"Did you feel that?"

"Yes."

"Didn't you know that eyelashes could speak? Which am I saying now—yes or no?"

He put both his arms round her. The darkness was total. The silence seemed to be a weight that he could feel. Her lips were ready for his; he could not have told whether it was his arms that drew her close, or her arms which bound them together. When he freed her lips, she used them to explore his cheeks, his forehead, his chin, before resting them once again upon his mouth. When at last she laid her head against him, she could hear his heart pounding.

"Funny how you didn't know about eyelashes," she said after a time. "What else don't you know?"

"Why you did that."

"I did it because I wanted to. I wanted to see how fast your heart could gallop. It's galloping like a Derby winner. Aren't you used to this combination of girl and darkness?"

"No. Nell—"

"Don't talk. I like you the way you are—just holding me."

A long time later, she stirred and sighed. "Is it long past dinner time?" she asked.

"Yes."

"Then I guess I'll have to call Corinne and tell her. Where's a phone?"

"We could stop at the house—I've got to put the car in the garage."

"No, not the house. We'll leave the car somewhere else, and I'll call her."

He took her to the telephone booth outside the post office in the square. Standing beside her, he could hear Corinne's voice raised sharply.

"I don't get it. You were out with him all morning, and you were swimming with him and you had tea at the summerhouse. Doesn't that add up to enough?"

"I just wanted to tell you—"

"I suppose you know what you're doing. I would have said that after the morning and the afternoon and the—"

Irritation rose suddenly in Nell, but she spoke calmly. "Suppose you let me write my own diary," she suggested. "I just didn't want you to wait dinner for me, that's all."

"Dinner was an hour ago. Haven't you eaten?"

"Not yet."

"Well, I could give you some good advice, but I don't suppose you'd take it."

"No. But thanks just the same."

She put the receiver down and looked at Hallam. "You're not liked around here," she told him. "My great-aunt warns me, my cousin warns me. My own good sense warns me. So what do I do?"

"You come with me"—Hallam led her out into the square and opened the door of the car—"to a summerhouse I know, where there's a man who can produce a wonderful dinner out of expensive cans."

"And after that?"

"After that"—he put the car into gear—"after that, who knows?"

CHAPTER

8

Mrs. Saltry was not a woman who believed in suffering in silence. But that night, tossing sleeplessly, she came to the reluctant conclusion that this was not a situation on which she would be wise to comment. Her instinct, as well as her usual practice, was to clear up matters by talking them over, but in this matter she had a feeling that she would talk too much and Nell would say nothing at all.

In love? It was impossible, she told herself, punching her pillow and wishing it were Hallam. Nell wouldn't go overboard as her mother had done; her head was cooler, she had more sense, more balance. All she was doing, all she and Hallam were doing, was filling in time. Matthew Berg, she remembered, hadn't needed much time, but he had been in a strong position—a rich man going after a girl who had nothing but a title. Hallam Grant wasn't poor, but he must realize that he would appear in a poor light if he tried to rush a rich girl like Nell off her feet. He wouldn't be after her money, but it would look that way, which came to the same thing. So why worry? This weather made it natural for them to spend their time in the lake or near the lake or wherever it was they spent it when they weren't swimming or sunbathing. What they did so late at night was anybody's guess and their own business. The good weather couldn't last much longer; rain was overdue, and when it came, it would dampen things down. Perhaps.

There were compensations, she admitted towards morning. She would rather be in Chenco than be here, but as she had made up her mind to stick it out until Nell was ready to leave, she might as well enjoy what there was to enjoy. Cosmo, for example. He was everything she looked for in a man—a man of his age: gentle, courteous, kind, eager to please and grateful for her society. And there was Miss Dell, for whom she felt sorry and to whom she had rashly offered coffee and whenever she cared to stop for it after delivering the office letters to Cosmo. Nothing like Miss Dell had ever been seen in Chenco; Miss Dell made up for a lot.

Meeting Nell on her way to her bath the next morning, she made a brief apology.

"I'm sorry I sounded like a cow mooing for its calf on the phone last night," she said. "It was the cook in me—I made some nice meat pies, and you didn't show up to eat them."

"I'm sorry, too," said Nell. "I didn't know it had gotten so late."

"That's what I thought. Have you left any hot water?"

"Heaps. Want me to make your coffee?"

"No, thank you. Run away and play with your boyfriend."

And that, she thought, shutting herself into the bathroom, was a nice touch—nothing anyone could pick on, but it gave some idea of what she was thinking. Feeling better, she turned on the hot tap.

Miss Dell arrived with a scarf tied round her hat to prevent it from being blown off as, head down, legs pedalling furiously, she sped across the Manor grounds to avoid encountering the governess cart. She was deeply grateful for

Mrs. Saltry's hospitality, and did her best to return it by regaling her with the history of her life in serial form.

"Well, yes, I do get lonely sometimes," she admitted when Mrs. Saltry questioned her, "but who doesn't? And I have so many resources—just think: my stamp collection, my needlework, the books I get out of the library, my work with Mr. Brierley—the days flash by, you know."

Mrs. Saltry pushed the sugar bowl nearer, and Miss Dell helped herself to a very small spoonful.

"If you feel like going to any concerts while you're here," she said, "I shall be only too glad to take you."

"Concerts? Here in Rivering?"

"Indeed, yes. We have had a symphony orchestra here for many, many years. All very gifted amateurs. They fill the Church Hall, which seats more than four hundred people. Are you musical?"

"No. I like to listen, but I don't perform. More coffee?"

"No, thank you. I can't tell you what a pleasure it is to drop in like this and have a few moments' chat with you. I shall miss you very much when you go." Miss Dell rose. "Is there anything I can bring you from the town when I come tomorrow?"

"Nothing at all, thank you very much."

"You will let me know, won't you, if Mr. Brierley wants anything? He would never ask for himself."

"I'll certainly let you know."

The days passed quickly, settling into a pleasant, unchanging pattern. After Miss Dell's morning visit, Mrs. Saltry invariably went shopping, accompanied as often as not by Mr. Moulton, who explained that the weather was so warm that he had insisted on his wife's taking the car. He was always impeccably groomed, perhaps in protest, conscious or unconscious, against his wife's daily uniform of drab, ill-cut jodhpurs. Mrs. Saltry was back at the house in time to prepare lunch, which Cosmo always came to share—a cold meal, so artistically presented that only as tea time approached did he realize how empty he felt. They ate at the table in Hallam's small garden; after lunch, Cosmo withdrew in order to allow Mrs. Saltry to have a rest. At tea time he was back again, with an offering of biscuits or one of the famous orange cakes from the town. Then it was her turn to visit his house. He had worked hard to tidy it up, rearranging the sofa and chairs so that they covered the stains on the carpet, even dusting the ornaments on the tables. He had not had much success at washing the windows; he had used either too little or too much detergent, and there were streaks which the curtains could not hide. But Mrs. Saltry seemed to notice no defects; she congratulated him on the wide variety of bottles now lined up on the table near the sofa, and taught him how to mix her favourite drink. He put out olives and almonds and little cheese biscuits and was careful to place the little dishes at her elbow, within reach. Towards the end of the week, his self-confidence had risen to the point at which he did not even remember to push his slippers under the sofa. He found it hard to believe that in his drawing room an elegant, charming woman sat contentedly listening, actually listening to his conversation. He found himself talking of his boyhood, of his happy bachelor days, of the opening of the commercial school next door to his office, and his meeting with and subsequent marriage to its principal.

"What was her name?" Mrs. Saltry asked.

"Thelma. She was not young, but she was very handsome. Everybody admired her."

"Did you fall in love with her right away?"

"Fall . . . oh, dear me, no. No, no. It wouldn't have occurred to me that . . . I wouldn't have dreamed that she would . . . she was so handsome, so—"

"You're rather handsome, yourself. How come you hadn't been snapped up before she came along?"

"Snapped . . . good gracious, what an idea! Who would

want to snap me up? I was a penniless lawyer. I couldn't afford to have an office in a better part of the town—she felt that very keenly. I lived in rather shabby rooms. I was happy, but how could I ask a woman to consider me as a husband?"

"Then how did you get Thelma to consider you?"

"Thelma? She was . . . well, she was next door to the office, and there were frequent occasions on which she needed advice. She used to come and see me, and then she invited me to visit her—she lived on the top floor of the commercial school building. She was . . . it was very neat. I may say scrupulously neat, nothing ever out of place. She was very shocked, very shocked, indeed, when she saw the rooms I lived in."

"What shocked her?"

"My bachelor habits. I am not a very tidy person, Mrs. Saltry."

"Corinne. Did Thelma try to make you tidier?"

"She determined to make me tidier, and she succeeded. I'm afraid that when she died, I fell below her standards. But I have never, if I may tell you this, never been able to understand the reason for constantly putting things away after use. If you use something which is not in normal use— valuable china, if you have it, which you perhaps take out in honour of a special guest—certainly you would put that away again. But things in daily use—things you use every morning, every evening . . . must you go to a cupboard, open it, take out plates, use them, wash them, dry them, replace them? Why? And dusting . . . do you know what happens when you use a duster? Some of the dust goes into the duster and is shaken out of the window—but the rest, I think the greater part of it, rises into the air and then slowly settles where it was before. What harm does it do to leave it un-disturbed? If you do not disturb it, you do not breathe it. Perhaps you don't agree with this?"

"There's a lot of sense in it," Mrs. Saltry declared. "But

even if there wasn't, when you're in your own house, why can't you keep it the way you like it? I like to put things away, but if you don't, who's going to tell you you should? People should leave people alone. I don't mean alone, I mean they should let them handle things the way they want to."

This, said with warmth and sincerity, seemed to Cosmo a proof of what he already suspected: that this was a woman in a million. He drew a deep sigh of content and refilled her glass. To take him as she found him . . . why couldn't Thelma have done that? Why should Mrs. Moulton have spread stories in the town labelling his house a pigsty? If a pigsty, would this well-groomed, fastidious woman visit it, or him?

So pleased was he to have so much of her company, that it was almost the end of the week before he noticed that they had had scarcely any of Nell's.

"Has Nell been visiting Lady Laura?" he asked.

"Twice." Mrs. Saltry's tone was dry. "But she's not interested in Lady Laura. Haven't you noticed? She spends all her time with Hallam Grant."

Cosmo's eyes rested on her in perplexity. "Don't you like him?"

"There's nothing to like or dislike. He's just one of those big, half-handsome men who seem to have a way with girls, that's all. I think she's crazy to spend so much time with him, but she's old enough to know what she's doing, and she's got a good enough head to know where it's leading."

"Do you mean that you don't want it to lead anywhere?"

She stared at him in astonishment. "Lead anywhere? Heavens, you don't want her to come over to Europe and fall for the first man she meets, do you?"

"Her mother—"

"I know. But Nell's got both feet on the ground. I hope."

"Hallam is a fine type," Cosmo pointed out mildly. "He seems to be doing well in his profession, and . . ."

"I'm glad. I hope he keeps right on doing well in his profession. I just don't see what it has to do with Nell, that's all. I can't say much to her—what can you say to a girl of her age? If she isn't grown-up now, she never will be. What I'd like to do is have a word or two with Hallam Grant—if I ever got to see him. But he's keeping out of my way."

At the end of the week, her resolution to let the affair take its course had worn thin, while her curiosity had grown to torturing proportions. Coming down and finding Nell—for once—still in the house, she greeted her in a voice she fought to keep light, but in which she could hear sharpness.

"Well, look who's here! No plans for today?"

Nell smiled. "Yes. I'm going to the Manor."

"That's a good idea. You might ask your aunt how much longer it's going to take her to pick out that memorial site. Then we can pack up and go home." She measured coffee into the coffeepot, spilling most of it on the table, and then spoke in an exasperated voice. "I wish I knew what was going on."

"If anything is."

"If anything is. You're with Hallam morning, noon and most of the night. You've been walking with him, driving with him, and swimming with him. You might be putting in time, but isn't it an awful lot of time?"

"Ten days. Is that an awful lot of time?"

"Nell, you're not getting yourself into anything, are you?"

"Such as what?"

"Don't stall. Not with me. You've got me worried sick. If this talk of memorials hadn't come up, we could have been on our way home now. I've seen you playing around with boys sometimes, but this man's different. Suppose you keep on monkeying around till you really fall in love— what happens then?"

"You tell me."

"All right, I will. Nothing happens, because it's got no future. His life's here and your life's where we came from.

I know geography doesn't come into it in ninety-nine cases out of a hundred, but this time it's really a case of two into one won't go. He's a kind of scholar, studying part of his time and digging part of his time and writing part of his time. Where would you fit in, if you were thinking of fitting in?"

"You're telling me, aren't you?"

"Yes. You don't—fit in. I don't see what you see in him, but I don't want to see him hurt, and I don't want to see you putting your head into something you can't get it out of again. I've been young. I know what a lake with a new moon over it looks like. I know what swimming in the dark feels like. I know what happens when two people as attractive as you both are think they can bring out a new set of safety rules. Why not get your mind onto your own affairs, Nell? Think about home. Think of getting on a plane and flying west and getting back to Chenco and driving out to the ranch and being welcomed in a way that'll warm your heart. And if that doesn't make you want to see about reservations, think about me. I want to go home."

"I know. You've been marvellous and I'm grateful."

"Fine. Then can we go?"

"Yes."

"When?"

Nell hesitated. "When Lady Laura's found what she wants, and I've handed over the money to pay for it."

"Is that a promise?"

"No. It's a plan. You can stop worrying about me."

Mrs. Saltry went dejectedly on with the preparations for her coffee. "Then I can start worrying about Cosmo," she said.

"Do you have to?"

"No, but nobody else does. Not a soul. There isn't a single person who takes any interest in whether he's comfortable or uncomfortable. He sits there in that awful room of his, making pathetic attempts to cover up all the mess, and not one word of complaint about the way he's been left to get along alone."

"Hallam says he likes getting along alone."

"Then Hallam's wrong. Men need someone to look after them. The more you hear about that wife Cosmo had, the more you understand why he looks the way he does, all timid and resigned. I don't know how I can listen to him the way I do, without opening my mouth and telling him what she really was—chasing after him from the commercial school she ran, keeping at him till she got him and then trying to make him over. It makes me boil."

Nell, listening, felt grateful to Cosmo for providing a counter-irritation. She spent the next hour house cleaning, and then went towards the Manor, only to find no pennant in view. She turned back and joined Hallam at the summer-house.

"Out," she told him.

"Good. What do you want to do today?"

"Anything you say. I'm in the mood for making the most of things while they last."

"What makes you think they're not going to last?"

She sat beside him on the hammock and rubbed her head against his shoulder. "Oh, Hallam, don't make it too hard. You know it can't go on."

"If you're talking about—"

"I'm talking about us. Corinne's right; we've been—"

"What, in God's name, does Corinne have to do with anything?"

"She's worried."

"What about?"

"Me. Give her her due; she hasn't said anything, and it's been killing her. She likes to come right out with things, but this time, she hasn't. That shows how hard she's taking it."

"She's anxious to get you back to America to marry you off to that son of hers. It's time I explained to her that I've assumed responsibility for you. And while I'm at it, I shall tell her to mind her own damned business."

"It's no use swearing. We've just got to be sensible, that's all."

"Sensible?" He put a hand under her cheek, raised her head and stared at her. "What's the matter with you? Are we or are we not in love? I'll put that another way. I love you. You said, quite clearly, and more than once, that you loved me. This morning, for no reason that I can see, you bring up Corinne."

"I talked with her this morning. I said I'd go home with her as soon as this thing of Lady Laura's gets settled."

"Then you've got to tell her you made a mistake. You've got to explain that circumstances have arisen which make it impossible for you to return with her. If she wants to go, let her."

"And then what do I do?"

"You stay here. Where else? Hasn't that been implicit all through these past ten days?"

"What's implicit?"

"Never mind. Keep to the point. What have you been doing for the past ten days—experimenting?"

"No."

"Then why the hell stroll up and announce that it's time you went home? What did you do—hire me by the week? Good God, do you think you can turn anything off now? If you want to go home, it's too late. You've made too many commitments this end. Me, for one. You're the girl who claimed to be able to communicate without words, remember? Well, there haven't been words, but there has been communication. Last night you were . . . what's got into you? Why don't you say something?"

"Why don't you stop shouting?"

"All right. I've stopped. Now explain this sudden change of front."

"There's no change of front. I have to go home sometime, don't I?"

"Certainly—at some future date. Nobody supposes that you've left your native land forever. All I'm pointing out is that you can't go back and leave things—things between us —in a half-finished state. You felt it reasonable to wait until your aunt finished her little bit of memorial business. It's more reasonable, it's natural, it's essential for you to finish our business, too. We have to become engaged. You have to visit my parents. We have to arrange our wedding. I have to hand over my revised book to the publishers. When we're married, I want to take you along to see what my brother Rowland is doing—that can be your introduction to archaeology. I've got professional colleagues I want you to meet. When all these things have been taken care of, we shall go back to your ranch and you can clear things up there and hand over to Master Saltry."

"Are you through?"

"For the moment."

"Then listen to me. I love you, but what's the use of going on? You and I are as different as two people could ever be. Corinne said so this morning, but she wasn't saying anything I didn't know. Do you think I haven't thought about it, trying to work it out? You don't know a thing about any of the things I was brought up with, and I don't know anything about what you do. You don't know about ranches and I'd be lost standing around watching you digging."

"How much would it matter to you if you never saw the ranch again?"

"It would matter a whole lot."

"How much would it matter to you if you never saw me again?"

"That's . . . that's silly."

"Yes, it's silly. But it's something you've got to face if you're ever going to know your own mind. You can't dis-

(183)

cuss love and marriage in the childish terms you've been using. What's between us is the only thing that counts."

"But I have to go home, don't you see that? I have to go home to find out how much this thing between us means."

"You're too late. You can no longer talk about going away —to think it over or for any other reason. You should have gone away ten days ago—if you'd wanted to. You're in with both feet, and I'm going to see that you stay in. There's not the smallest necessity for you to go back at this point, with or without Corinne. Your place—until we're married— is in England. You've learned enough about me to know I'm no great catch, but I'm sound. My parents are sound, my job's sound, my prospects are more than sound. If you want to go on being rich, there's nothing to stop you, but you won't find much to spend your money on until our children start coming. This thing has happened quickly, but there are no unseen snags. I've never been seriously involved— certainly I've never wanted to marry a girl—until I saw you. I'm offering you a good life, even if you find it strange at the beginning. I shouldn't be surprised at your having these second thoughts, because I knew that some kind of reaction was bound to set in—but I'm not going to let you go back to America, to sit on your ranch tossing dollars to decide whether you will or will not return to me. There'll be no problem about returning, because you're not going to leave."

"Suppose I said I wasn't sure I was really in love?"

"You'd be lying." He put his arms round her, set the hammock swinging gently, and held her close. "What are you afraid of, Nell? You may have acted impulsively, but it was a good impulse. When you marry me, you'll have two homes instead of one. You can take our children to the ranch and teach them to ride. All you have to remember now, all you have to hang on to, is the fact that we love one another."

"Yes, but—"

"Leave the buts to Corinne; she'll think of dozens. What

does she know about marriage? If you have to take three shots at it, you can't claim to be an expert. You and I are going to be like my parents—like your parents would have been if your mother had lived—growing closer all the time. I promise to take care of you—all my life. Do you believe that?"

"Yes."

"Then you can stop listening to Corinne. Tell her to go on mothering Cosmo." He paused. "What she has to say about us is nothing to what Lady Laura's going to say when we tell her."

"She won't care either way, will she? I'm nothing to her."

"With Stapling blood in your veins? She'll bring out her heaviest ammunition."

"When do we tell her?"

"You don't. I do. But not today, because I've just remembered why the flag's not flying. I met Banks, who told me she'd gone up to London for the day. So you can spend the day with me. Today and every day."

There was no further mention of Mrs. Saltry, but Hallam walked with Nell to his house that evening, and while she went upstairs to change into a dress in which to go out and dine with him, he waited in the drawing room and—as he had expected—Mrs. Saltry came in with the air of a woman determined to speak her mind.

"I was hoping to see you," she told him. "Did Nell tell you that I'd been talking to her about going home?"

"She did."

"Let me say straight out that her future is her own affair, and I'm not trying to interfere. All I don't like is this rush treatment you've been giving her. I said she ought to come home with me, and she agreed."

"It was a silly suggestion," he said mildly.

"You have a better one?"

"Yes. To stay here and marry me, and go home when we've tidied things up this end."

"What makes you think you can offer her the kind of life she's led in the past?"

"She doesn't want to lead the life she's led in the past. Married to me, she starts a new life."

"What do you two have in common?"

"Everything that matters."

"Look, Hallam"—she did her best to sound reasonable—"I've nothing against you as a man, only as a husband for Nell. Try to see it from my angle: if you were in my place, would you just smile and say Bless the Bride—and go away and leave her?"

"If she had found a man she loved, a man capable of making her a good husband, I would go away happy in the certainty that she's going to be happy."

"How do I know anything about you, except by guessing—or taking your word for it? All I've seen you do is lie in a hammock. I can see that you're big and upstanding and good-looking, as looks go—but I could name a dozen men in Chenco who could give her everything you've got, and—"

"—throw in some horses. Has Nell met this desirable dozen, or were you keeping them as a surprise for her?"

"If you mean you're the first man that's really lit the fuse, you're right—but all the same, why can't you give her time? Where's the rush? She goes back home, she thinks it over, and she comes back—if she wants to. Who's going to stop her?"

"You'd do your best."

"Is that what you're afraid of?"

"No. I'd stake everything on her coming back to me— but the point I'm trying to make is that having fallen in love, having decided to marry me, there's a shift in focus. The future takes precedence over the past."

"She's got big responsibilities over there, can't you see that? She's the head, whether she wants to be or not, of a huge enterprise. She's the boss. She has, I can't tell you how many, people depending on her. Before she marries anybody, she has to talk to people—her friends, her godparents, her banker, her lawyer. How I see it is that you're just being mulish, taking a stand and refusing to change your mind even if it's for Nell's good. What does it sound like when I go back to Chenco and they ask me where Nell is and I tell them she met this fellow and in less than two weeks decided to marry him? Does that sound like sense? I know her mother fell in love just as soon as she saw Matthew Berg, but she had enough time afterwards to think, to know what she wanted, to decide. You're not giving Nell time for anything. I wish she'd never met you." She turned to the door as Nell entered. "I repeat that. I wish you'd never met him. And now you can both go away and let me have a good howl."

"Oh, Corinne"—Nell looked at her helplessly—"do you have to take it this way?"

"Yes, I do." Mrs. Saltry dabbed angrily at her eyes and then faced Hallam. "Are you going to tell Lady Laura about this?"

"I'm going to do more than tell her. I'm going to ask her permission. She's Nell's nearest relation."

Mrs. Saltry turned to Nell. "You've really made up your mind to stay here and marry him?"

"Yes. I wish you'd believe we know what we're doing."

Mrs. Saltry stared out of the window. Two tears trickled down her cheeks. She ignored them.

"When you come to my age," she said, "when you've seen as much of men as I have, you get to thinking they're all pretty much of a kind. You don't know anything about Hallam, but you don't get to know anything that matters before you're married. So I guess picking a stranger doesn't matter much in the long run. All I wanted you to do was to go home first, that's all, and if you think I'm thinking of Jack, you're dead right. I am. Now will you please go away? I'd like to cry."

"You could celebrate instead," Hallam suggested. "Dinner for four, on me. If you'll come, I'll go and get Cosmo."

Mrs. Saltry looked at him. Her eyes were moist, but when she had dried them, an approving light shone through. "That's the first sensible thing you've said since you came in," she told him. "Go and get Cosmo while I put on a celebration gown."

If it was not a celebration, it was a good dinner in pleasant surroundings—a roadhouse two miles from Rivering, backed by a sheltered garden in which tables had been set out. Cosmo insisted on being host, and ordered champagne to drink a toast to Nell and Hallam.

When they rose to leave, Mrs. Saltry's eyes rested in surprise on an elderly man who was walking with a woman to the door.

"Look, Nell," she said. "Recognize him?"

"Yes. Mr. Slasenger," Nell said.

"Friend of yours?" Hallam asked her.

"No. Corinne talked with him at our hotel in Paris and he took us out to dinner."

"He was waiting for his wife to join him," Mrs. Saltry said. "I guess that's who she is. They look married."

"You mean it shows?" Hallam asked.

"After a long time, I guess it does. People get to look like couples. Do you suppose they're staying in Rivering?"

"Why don't you ask them?" Hallam suggested.

"They're too far away, and it isn't worth it. Look, they're getting into a taxi."

They drove back to Stapling. Hallam left Mrs. Saltry and Cosmo at his house, and Nell went with him to garage the car.

"Do you know what I'd like to do now?" she asked.

"No. Tell me."

"I'd like to swim. There's a moon, and it's warm, and you heard what Cosmo said about the weather?"

"Yes. Rain on the way."

"Do you want to swim?"

"No. But I want to immerse myself, and you, in the lake and float, looking up at that moon. You told me that wasn't swimming."

"It isn't—but let's do it."

He took her hand, and they walked slowly towards the still, moonlit water.

CHAPTER

9

The next morning, Hallam discussed with Nell his plan of going to see Lady Laura to tell her of their engagement—a plan which was destined never to be carried into effect. Nell was in favour of their going together, but Hallam preferred the idea of a formal approach made by himself alone.

"Why won't you take me with you?" she asked.

"Let's say I want to draw her fire. Anyway, it's a nice gesture, asking her permission."

"It doesn't mean anything."

"She'll have to make some kind of comment, and I'm interested to know what it'll be. The first salvo, of course, will be that I'm marrying you for your money. I shan't deny it."

"Why not?"

"Because, having so keen a nose for money herself, she'll probably put it down as a mark in my favour."

"You're sure it wouldn't be better if we both went?"

"Quite sure. I'll go at eleven. You can go down to Rivering in my car and buy something for lunch. See those clouds gathering up there? We'll have a picnic, but it'll be the last for some time, if the weather reports mean anything."

Nell drove to the town and left the car in the parking lot next to the hotel. She had finished her shopping and was on the way back to the car when she heard her name spoken.

"Miss Berg!"

She turned to find Mr. Slasenger standing outside the hotel beside his wife, adjusting his glasses in order to see her more clearly.

"It *is* Miss Berg," he said. "Well now, isn't that a coincidence, finding you here? Francie, this is a young lady who was at the hotel I stayed in in Paris. This is my wife, Miss Berg. Where is your cousin? Is she here in Rivering with you?"

"She's staying—we're both staying in a house up on the hill. I think I saw you at a restaurant last night. Are you going to be here long?"

"No." It was Mrs. Slasenger who answered. She was short and plump and smiling, with gray hair that was too luxuriant, too permanently set to be anything but a wig. "As a matter of fact, we're going back to London right after lunch. We only came"—she stopped and turned to her husband—"you'd better tell it, Clem, unless you think we hadn't better say anything."

"It's not a secret, Francie. It was just that she didn't want it mentioned in this town. She didn't want to be bothered by people asking to see all that lovely furniture she has." He turned to Nell. "It's a present I've bought for my wife, Miss Berg. I think I told you, over in Paris, that my wife was going to join me for our fiftieth wedding anniversary. I wanted to find a special present to give her—and I found one."

"Here in Rivering?" Nell asked.

"Yes." Mrs. Slasenger nodded. "Here in Rivering. But we heard about it in London. Go ahead and tell it, Clem."

"A dealer in London told me I might be able to get what I'd been looking for if I came down here," Mr. Slasenger explained. "He offered to put me in touch with a lady living here, who maybe had just what I wanted. The first time, I came down alone—I didn't want to disappoint Francie if I didn't find anything good enough. But I did find something. I found just what I wanted. I didn't hesitate one instant. I closed the deal right away, but there was no deal, the owner said, until I had taken the box—it's a box, Miss Berg, but a very special kind of box—until I had taken it to London, to any expert I wanted, to have it certified as genuine. So that's what I did. And it's genuine—and it's ours. If you had a minute to spare, we'd like to have you come up and see it."

"I . . . thank you." Nell wondered whether the heat was affecting her brain. A box was merely a box, wasn't it? There were dealers in this town, weren't there? She cleared her throat. "If it's not too much bother—"

"Oh, no bother, no bother at all," Mrs. Slasenger assured her. "It's a real pleasure. We'll go up to our hotel room. We've only been here one night," she said on their way up in the elevator. "It's kind of small, but nice for a short stay. Clem, did you bring the key?"

"I have it right here." He opened the door and ushered them into the room. "The cardboard wrapping is only temporary, Miss Berg; that's just a way of keeping the box from scratching till I can get it properly packed in London. I want to take good care of it—it's a real treasure."

Nell waited. He did not take long to undo the string. The thick fold of cardboard opened, revealing the box inside. It was the Bible box.

"It's beautiful, isn't it?" breathed Mrs. Slasenger. "And genuine. Absolutely genuine."

Nell could only look. Her silence, added to a certain quality of stillness in her attitude, was highly gratifying to the new owners.

"You see, Clem? It's so beautiful, people don't know what to say. I can't wait to get home and show it to the folks."

"Yes, it's beautiful." Nell came out of her trance. "Was there any trouble about getting the owner to sell it?"

"She didn't want to part with it, and you can see why," Mr. Slasenger said. "But you know how it is—people find that money doesn't have the value they thought it had, and old ladies like this one who sold this to us have to let something go if they want to go on being comfortable. I felt real sorry for her, but a bargain's a bargain, and she came out of it all right financially. She didn't cheat, and I didn't cheat; she wouldn't sell it until I'd had it certified as genuine, and when I paid, I paid her price without haggling."

Nell thanked them again, left them in their room, went down in the elevator and found herself in the square without knowing how she got there. She found that certain facts were going round and round in her brain: up to London to keep in touch with values—that made sense, now. Up to London to find buyers, back to Stapling to sell property that did not belong to her. . . .

She took the main road up to the Manor, found herself swinging round a corner too fast, and tried to control her fury. She stopped at the bridge, got out of the car and glanced upwards. No pennant. She was out. But at the door of the Manor stood the hired car she used for journeys beyond the scope of the governess cart; she had not yet left.

Banks admitted her, told her that Lady Laura was out in the governess cart, but would be back shortly in order to go by car to a luncheon engagement in London. He conducted her to the drawing room and left her.

There was not much room between the furniture to pace, but Nell paced—up and down, up and down. Her eyes went round the room and she tried to assess how much would be missing if the contents could be checked against the list that

Cosmo had made. How much had gone? Her aunt had protested that she could not, would not bring herself to sell—but she had sold. Down there, at the hotel, was the beautiful Bible box which had belonged to her mother, which now belonged to herself, which she had wanted to buy, and been refused. There it had stood, on that table over there. . . .

She stopped. Feet, brain, faculties seemed to halt simultaneously. It had been there, on that table . . . and it was still there. The Bible box was there, where it had always been. But it was also down at the hotel, wrapped in protective cardboard. . . .

Genuine? They had had it inspected by an expert. It was genuine—they had said so. Then what was this? What was anything in this room, in these rooms? Copies, replicas, fakes, shams? Had her aunt been selling the genuine pieces and living with the reproductions?

She heard the clang of the bell. She turned and ran out of the room and down to the hall. She would have flung open the great door if Banks had not reached it first. On the threshold was not Lady Laura, but Hallam.

"Good morning, Banks. May I come in and wait for Lady Laura? I—" He saw Nell and broke off in surprise, which turned to apprehension as he saw her expression. "What's happened?"

"Come up here." She flung the words over her shoulder as she went up the stairs. He was on her heels as she reached the top. She swung round to face him.

"You said she didn't sell things. She does. She has."

"Steady." He was scarcely listening; his eyes were on her white, set face. "Don't worry, she won't sell anything of value."

"She did. She has. The Bible box."

His eyes went past her and rested on it. "Darling Nell, turn round. It's there, behind you."

"That's not the real one. The real one's at the hotel. She sold it to Mr. Slasenger and his wife. Remember him, them?

They were at the restaurant last night. They came to Rivering to bring back the Bible box, which they'd taken up to London, to an expert. The expert said it was genuine, and they bought it. I saw it in their room at the hotel—they took me up and unwrapped the cardboard and there it was. They're leaving after lunch, taking it with them. So you were wrong. Cosmo was wrong. She lied. She does sell things. I wanted that Bible box. That was all I wanted, and she said I couldn't have it. I would have bought it, she knows I would, but she sold it to . . . to strangers. She let it go. She—"

"Nonsense," Hallam broke in, and the conviction in his voice silenced her. "Nonsense. There's a piece missing."

"I've just told you so. The Bible box."

"I'm not talking about furniture; I'm talking about fitting pieces of a puzzle together."

"Where's the puzzle? Can't I believe my own eyes?"

"Not this time. I said, and I repeat; she wouldn't sell any of her treasures."

"My treasures. Maybe it's because they're mine that she can bring herself to part with them."

"She regards them as her own. She wouldn't sell anything. I don't know her well, but I know she's a fanatic about two things: her Stapling blood and the Stapling possessions. She wouldn't sell."

"But she *did*, Hallam, she *did*. Go down to the hotel and look for yourself. She . . ."

"She's coming," Hallam said.

They stood listening to the slow footsteps. Banks opened the door and Lady Laura came in. When the door closed, she stood still, waiting to recover her breath. Hallam pushed a chair forward, and she sank onto it.

"I do not object to Ellen waiting for me when I am out," she said at last, "but I—"

"The Bible box," Nell broke in. "You sold it."

There was no sound for some moments. The only movement was that of Lady Laura's head, which turned slowly to Hallam and then back to Nell.

"I don't care to discuss family matters before strangers," she said.

"I'm not really a stranger," Hallam explained. "I came here to tell you that Nell and I are engaged. I found her here in the state in which you see her now."

"I've met Mr. Slasenger before," Nell said. "I met him again down in Rivering just now, with his wife. They told me about a box they'd bought. They took me up to their room at the hotel, and showed it to me. They said it was genuine, because they'd had it looked at by an expert in London. I came here to ask you about it, and while I was waiting for you, I saw . . . the other box on the table. So what I think I would like you to tell me is how much of all this"—her gesture took in the contents of the room—"is fake."

Lady Laura's face showed nothing but a faint distaste. "I think I told you the first, or perhaps the second time we met, that I had—perhaps I didn't use the words—a ruling passion."

"You said you wouldn't sell anything—but you did. You have."

"Yes. I sell things, from time to time."

"And you sold the Bible box, the one I wanted to take home with me, the one that belonged to my mother. You wouldn't even let me buy it—but you sold it to them, the Slasengers."

Hallam's eyes had not left Lady Laura.

"Or you didn't," he said quietly. "My bet is that you didn't."

"You win your bet—if you made it," Lady Laura told him. "I did not sell the Bible box."

"Then what has Mr. Slasenger got in his room at the hotel, wrapped up in cardboard?" Nell demanded.

"He has a Bible box. It is not genuine."

"But he took it to London, to an expert. He . . ."

"Will you sit down, please, both of you?" Lady Laura's voice sounded weary. "I shall explain, but there is no need for you to stand there like accusers. The facts are simple. I sell, from time to time, articles small enough to be carried, without trouble, in the luggage of travellers. I have already told you that the only people I admit to see my possessions are people from overseas—transatlantic, for the most part. I choose as customers—victims, if you prefer—people like the Slasengers, who are elderly and in Europe for a rare and probably sole visit—in their case, a fiftieth wedding anniversary. In other cases, it may be a round-the-world voyage after a man has retired from business. Mr. Boutin sends people like these to see my things. I do not offer to sell; I have to be persuaded. When something has been chosen, I insist on its being inspected by an expert and guaranteed genuine. The buyers return from London and I invite them to dine with me. I have ready in my room a replica of the article they have bought. After dinner, the sale is completed and I ring for Banks to bring stout wrapping paper and string. I wrap up the genuine article and then find I have no scissors to cut the string. I carry the article to my room, exchange the genuine for the replica and return to the drawing room. The buyers leave with the reproduction. They are completely satisfied with their purchase; I am completely satisfied with the price they have paid."

"But—"

"My dear Ellen." Lady Laura raised a languid hand. "Please allow me to finish. The buyers return to their homes and exhibit an article which they are convinced is absolutely genuine. Nobody but a true expert could detect any difference between the original and the copy. I still have my Bible box, and I also have some money to pay my bills. You are going to tell me that this is dishonest, that this amounts to cheating. It is and it does. But consider, please: tourists all over the world have always been, will always be cheated.

They ask to be cheated. They know, most of them, nothing whatsoever about values, yet they have the impertinence to bargain and to haggle. They pretend to a knowledge greater than that of the vendors. They are, more often than not, looking for something which they can take home to excite the greed and envy of their friends. Nothing in this world would induce me to part with my possessions. I have said this and I repeat it. But there is a certain satisfaction in sharing them in this way. Nobody, at this moment, can be happier than Mr. and Mrs. Slasenger. To rush to them, as you are no doubt longing to do, to expose me, to tell them, that they have been the victims of a fraud, to rob them of the delight they are feeling in their new purchase—do it if you must, but in my view you are bringing dark elements into a situation which at present has none. When I am dead, you will find here everything that was on the list made so long ago by Cosmo Brierley. It is all here, and if at some time you come across replicas in British Columbia or Indiana or Peru, you may assure yourself that they are, indeed, replicas. I am not surprised at your attitude. I am only surprised that you sat through the *son et lumière* episodes without rising to your feet to denounce them as false. When you are my age, you will understand that the lives of most people are lived behind what I may call a shop window. And now" —she rose slowly to her feet, so slowly that Hallam walked over to her and offered an arm, which she accepted—"you will have to excuse me. I am going to meet two people—not to sell them anything, but to buy something. One is a man with land which might be a suitable site for the Stapling memorial; the other is an architect to whom I wish to show the designs I have made for a possible building. Goodbye, Ellen. You are more like your mother than I realized. You, like her, allow your emotions to carry you beyond reason."

She held Hallam's arm on her way down the stairs. Nell, standing motionless, could hear the sounds of her departure —the car starting, the pause when it had driven away, the

closing of the great door, Hallam's footsteps as he came upstairs to join her. He walked up to her and took her in his
arms.

"Don't take it to heart," he begged. "I can't bear to see
you looking like this. She's done it before and she'll do it
again. All she said was right—according to her lights."

She freed herself. "I can't do it, Hallam." Her tone was
firm. "I can't, I can't, I *can't*."

"Can't do what?"

"I can't let those two go away without . . . oh, it's horrible!
She talks about pride, and cheats. She—"

"You mean you're going to tell them?"

"Yes. No. I *know* them. I don't mean that they're friends
of mine, but I've seen them, I've spoken to them. I know
they're a decent, friendly, harmless couple who never de-
served anything like this. They're going back home to exhibit a fake, and every time they tell their friends it's genuine, they'll be lying. Every single person who looks at it will
be one of the—the victims. Don't you see?"

"Yes, I see." He spoke calmly. "So you have two choices:
you go down and tell them the truth, or . . ."

"Or?"

"Or you see to it that the box they exhibit is the genuine
one."

"The . . . but how?"

"By doing exactly what she did: switching them."

She stared at him, open-mouthed.

"You're crazy," she said at last. "They've got it in their
room, wrapped up. They're leaving in two hours or less."

"Which means that we have to hurry. If it can be done,
do you want to do it? Think before you answer. If you let
them take away that box that's on the table behind you,
you're doing something your aunt never did: eating into
the collection. That box has come down to you through
the centuries; do you really want to hand it over to a couple
from nobody knows where? Do you?"

"Oh no, no, no! Of course I don't! But I can't live for the rest of my life knowing that I cheated people who don't deserve to be cheated. If I didn't *know,* I wouldn't have any responsibility—but I *do* know. This isn't a small thing; it's cheating on a big scale. It's fraud." She turned and picked up the box. "I'm going to let them have this."

"They'll never know the difference."

"*They* won't—but I will, and you will."

"And what about Lady Laura?"

"You mean . . . do we tell her? Of course we tell her—but not till the Slasengers have gone away and we've put the fake box on the table. Then we'll tell her."

"No, we won't. Look, Nell, I'll make a bargain with you. I'll make the switch—how, I don't know, but I'll do it somehow—but I won't do it unless you promise never to tell your aunt what we've done."

"But—"

"Think of it as Nemesis. Every time she looks at the box, she—"

"But next time she wants to cheat, next time someone takes it to London to be examined by an expert, the expert will say it's not genuine. So then what happens?"

"Then she'll engage in a battle royal to prove him wrong. Will you agree not to tell her?"

"If you like, but I can't see why you don't want her to know."

"But you won't tell her?"

"No."

"You're sure? You couldn't bear to practice deception on the Slasengers, who are complete strangers to you. Can you deceive Lady Laura, who's your own flesh and blood?"

"Yes, I can."

"Then God grant me insight into the workings of your mind. And now take off that jacket and sling it over your shoulders and put the box under your arm. Yes, like that. Don't let the jacket slip. We'll go down as quietly as we can, but if Banks hears us, he'll come into the hall to let us out, and I'd rather he didn't. Ready?"

They went swiftly and silently, closing the door behind them with as little noise as possible. They walked to the car, and Hallam got into the driver's seat.

"This may not work," he said, "but the fact that the Slasengers are going away helps. Were their things packed?"

"I didn't . . . yes. Their suitcases were filled, ready to close."

"And the box is wrapped in cardboard?"

"Yes."

"If they're not in their room, it'll be difficult. If they're up in their room, it'll be easy . . . easier. You go up, you ask if you left your scarf or gloves or parcels or . . . you can think of something. You ask them to go down and have a pre-lunch drink with you. You make an excuse, any excuse, to hold the key after they lock the door. I'll stand at the reception desk; your job will be to put the keys down where my hand happens to be. I can't do more than stand there, hoping. Once I get the key, the rest is easy. Do you still want to do this?"

"Yes."

"Then sit quiet and collect your thoughts until we get to the hotel."

The operation was accomplished so smoothly, so successfully, that Hallam said later that they had missed their vocation. Nell went up to the Slasengers' room, knocked on the door and asked if by any chance she had left a parcel behind. They found no parcel. She made the suggestion of a drink and allowed the Slasengers to talk her into accepting one from them. On the way to the elevator, she made a casual reference to the size and weight of the key ring that Mr. Slasenger was holding. He handed it to her, and she swung it for some moments and then changed the subject. With the key ring still in her hand, she stopped at the entrance to the bar and said she had forgotten to leave it at the desk.

Mr. Slasenger offered to go back, but she advised him to order the drinks instead. Her halt beside Hallam, her few words of greeting and surprise at seeing him, sufficed for the exchange of the key from her hand to his. She watched him as he walked to the elevator—this time it was his own jacket which swung from his shoulders, and she saw nothing to indicate that he was carrying anything under his arm.

He was waiting for her in the car when she came out of the hotel. She got in beside him and gave him an inquiring glance.

"Mission accomplished," he told her. "Now you can begin to express your regret at losing the Bible box."

"The mission isn't accomplished—we still have to get this other box back to the drawing room."

"Easy."

Easy it was. Banks came to the door and offered to go up and look for the parcel Nell thought she had left behind. She pointed out that she could go faster and with less fatigue; she came down without the parcel, Banks let them out and they walked to the car. They heard the door close behind them, and Nell stopped and took Hallam's hand.

"Thank you," she said.

"What for?"

"Why, for changing the boxes over."

"You're quite certain that I did change them over?"

"Of course you did. That's what you went up to their room to do—make the switch."

"But did I make it? You must keep asking yourself, because you will never really know. Would Hallam, you must ask yourself, now and forevermore, would Hallam have given up the real for the replica?"

"But . . . but didn't you?"

"Who will ever know? Which box is where? Are the Slasengers travelling to their home to deceive their friends or is their purchase genuine, as they believe? Is Lady Laura gloating over the original, or the reproduction?"

"But . . ."

"At times, when you love me, you will be certain that I did what you asked me to, and made the switch. At other times, when I ill-treat you, you will realize that there are dark depths in my character that you failed to plumb."

"Will you please talk sense?"

"You're going to marry me, aren't you?"

"Of course I am."

"After which, what's yours will be mine, including Bible boxes. Would I—this is what you must ask yourself—would I give up a genuine Bible box, so soon to be mine?"

"Hallam, *please* stop being silly. Did you make that switch?"

He bent and kissed her lingeringly.

"One of these days, if you're very, very good," he promised, "I'll tell you."

CHAPTER

10

The weather broke that afternoon in a thunderstorm so violent that it was to remain long in the memory of the people of Rivering. Thunder rolled, lightning flashed and rain fell relentlessly, flooding the market square and bringing traffic to a standstill.

Cosmo, recalling that Mrs. Saltry had admitted to being frightened of thunder, draped himself in a heavy mackintosh, put on a fishing hat and made his way through the downpour to Hallam's house to offer her his company. He was rewarded by her gratitude, spontaneous and sincere, and a glass of punch.

"There—that's to warm you," she said. "It was sweet of you to come. I was feeling kind of miserable. I hoped Nell would be back, but I haven't seen her all day."

"Is she with Hallam?"

"Why ask? Now and forever."

Cosmo put down his glass and looked at her, his face aglow with pleasure. "I'm delighted, really delighted," he said.

"Why? You don't know much more about him than Nell does, or than I do."

Cosmo's face fell. "You're disappointed," he said. "I can understand that—but you should be happy for her. It may seem very sudden to you, very hasty and rushed and so on, but you forget that I saw the meeting between her mother and—"

"—my cousin Matthew. I know."

"What did any of us know about him? It was all trust—trust in one's instincts, trust in the future . . ."

"All I wanted her to do was go home and clear her brain, that's all. But she wouldn't listen, and he wouldn't listen, and you sit there saying everything's going to be fine, but I still don't see that it's much of a life to offer Nell. What fun is it going to be for her, standing in maybe Egypt watching a lot of grown men scratching away at some mud and coming up with bits of broken jars? Oh, I know all about Tutankhamen. It took them three thousand years to locate him. What sort of life is that for a wife? I'm not saying there aren't hundreds if not millions of happy women married to archaeologists, but I didn't want Nell to be one of them. I wanted her to come home with me, but she's staying, so I'm going alone."

"I shall be very, very sorry to see you go," Cosmo told her.

"I'll be sorry, too. You know something, Cosmo? I've enjoyed these evenings with you more than I could ever tell you. It's been wonderful and I'm sorry it's over."

"Perhaps you'll come back one day and—"

"I don't see"—Mrs. Saltry spoke with sudden resolution —"I don't see why it *should* be over. Listen to me, Cosmo. Over there, I've got a great, big house. I've told you about it. I've shown you pictures. I've told you how I like to have people come and visit, and swim in the pool and eat and drink and even dance. Why don't you come and stay with me? Why don't you retire—you can retire any time you want to—and shut your house and get on a plane and come and see if my house lives up to its pictures? I can just see you over there." She half-closed her eyes and with her hands sketched the scene. "There's that beautiful patio, and two long chairs with green and yellow cushions and a little canopy, and you're lying there with a cool drink right beside you, just looking at the view and soaking up sun and getting to know everybody in Chenco." She opened her eyes and fixed them on him. "You've got to come. You've been too long in this place, worrying about old Lady Laura and what she's doing. You'll have nothing to do over there but enjoy yourself. I've got a fast car and I can take you places. I'll take good care of you. I won't let you out of my sight for a minute, and you'll grow nice and fat and lazy and you'll never, never want to move again. Will you come?"

He managed, with a great effort, to make a sound which she took, if not for assent, at least for gratitude. He tried to lever himself out of his chair, and found his legs strangely weak. The punch? Surely not; it was beside him, almost untouched. He put his hands on the chair arms and after two attempts, rose and walked slowly to the window. He could not see his house; between it and this one was a screen of rain. But he did not need to look out; he could look inward and with his mind's eye see plainly all that made his life so pleasant, all that was familiar and loved. Some of his things he had lately hidden away, but he knew where to find them, and suddenly he longed to bring them out once more, longed to have them round him again. There was no patio, no continual sunshine; his car was not fast and the only chair with comfortable cushions was shabby—but he had, he realized with an uprush of gratitude, everything he wanted in the world. Even the cloud which for so long had hung over him—the cloud of his inadequate trusteeship—had vanished. He was a free man. Free—not to go, but to stay.

He turned, and his gaze fell on Mrs. Saltry, who was pouring herself another drink. He stared at her back, his look no longer grateful, but haunted. How much, he wondered fearfully, had she read into those pleasant evenings? Had he said, had he done anything that could have misled her? The invitation she had tendered a few minutes ago—why should he suspect that it sprang from anything more than simple friendship? What had she said, what had she done to give him this feeling of near-panic? Was he incapable of thanking a woman for a kind thought, and saying that he would think over her offer?

Yes, he admitted miserably. He was. He was totally unable to make a stand. If she insisted—and he knew her to be a determined woman—what would he say? She was going to the travel agents to make reservations for herself; would she, could she go so far as to make them also for him, taking his acceptance for granted? He had no idea. He knew only that he wanted to get out of a room that suddenly seemed close and airless. Rain or no rain, he wanted to go out and take a long walk . . . alone.

She was turning to face him. He braced himself, his face very pale. But she did not renew the invitation. Her excitement, her enthusiasm had left her. She merely sighed, leaning against the table, glass in hand.

"You know something? I feel kind of old," she told him.

"Old?"

"That's right—old. I've never said that before, to anybody, because I've never felt it before. But I feel it now." She picked up his glass and handed it to him. "Let's drink to lots more summers."

He drank the toast, and then he found himself in the hall, fumbling for his sodden mackintosh. She made no attempt

(207)

to keep him; she helped him into the garment, and then opened the front door and leaned forward to drop a light kiss on his cheek.

"You've been very kind to me," he said humbly. "Thank you."

"You're easy to be kind to."

She closed the door after him and walked slowly back to the drawing room. There was nothing to do now but make the reservations, pack—and go home. There was no need to feel this way; the future would be more fun, not less fun; there would be Nell to visit in England, Nell's visits to the States to look forward to. Things hadn't changed; they'd just shifted round a bit, that was all. She still had her house, and her money, and her friends—what was there to moan about? Nothing.

In the morning, she was more herself, but a residue of depression remained and made her look with unwonted pleasure at the drab figure of Miss Dell, propping up her bicycle against the gate and hurrying up the path through the drizzle.

"Why, come in—you're all wet!" Mrs. Saltry exclaimed. "You're earlier this morning—and you've still got Mr. Brierley's letters. Leave them here; I'll see that he gets them."

"Good morning. Thank you," Miss Dell said. "I saw Mr. Brierley as I was coming here, but he was some way off, and I didn't want to stop in the grounds. But I must speak to him, because— Oh, I'm so sorry. I should have taken off my wet mackintosh before sitting in your nice chair. Please forgive me. I am a little nervous this morning."

"Well, here's some nice hot coffee. Drink that and dry off," Mrs. Saltry said.

Miss Dell was gulping, a great contrast to her usual manner of taking genteel sips.

"Has anything happened?" Mrs. Saltry asked.

"Yes." Miss Dell put down her cup and lowered her voice. "It may prove to be a very serious matter—one can never tell. This morning, I passed—I shall have to say that name —Lady Laura. She was standing outside the porch of the Manor, looking—I think—to see if it was too wet for her to go out. And above her, I saw . . . a shadow. You know, of course, what that means?"

Mrs. Saltry, for once, was at a loss for words. Miss Dell, during these morning visits, had more than once claimed to have seen shadows; the last one had resulted in someone missing a train.

"So what do you do now?" she asked.

Miss Dell shook her head firmly. "Myself, I do nothing. I could not bring myself to approach her personally. I am going to ask you to tell Mr. Brierley what I have told you. He is the person to warn her. Will you make quite sure that he gets the message?"

"Yes, I will. I'll tell him when I give him the letters. Will that be soon enough?"

"I hope, I trust so," Miss Dell said solemnly. "And now will you forgive me if I hurry away?"

She went into the hall. Mrs. Saltry followed her, and something in the angular, lonely figure went suddenly to her heart. What became of misfits like this? If anything happened to Cosmo, what would happen to Miss Dell?

"Look, Miss Dell, I've been packing. You know I'm going back to the States?"

Miss Dell's face clouded. "Not at once, surely?"

"Practically. And I'm going alone. Miss Berg is staying here."

"Oh! I shall miss you so much!" It was a cry of deep, genuine distress. "You've been so kind to me—and more important, you've been so kind to Mr. Brierley. I shall never forget you." Miss Dell fumbled for her handkerchief. "I shall—"

"What I was going to ask," Mrs. Saltry broke in hastily, "was whether you know someone I could give some of my things to—the things I don't want to take back with me. Maybe you have friends who wouldn't mind. . . . The dresses are almost new, and there are two pairs of shoes, and . . . well, things like that. I'll bring them down here and you can go through them and see if there's anything anybody could use."

Sitting on the stairs, they went through the pile. Miss Dell's cheeks grew pink and her eyes shone; she fingered pleats, stroked the beautiful materials and tried on the shoes. The fiction about friends was forgotten.

"Would you think me terribly selfish if I kept them for myself?" she asked Mrs. Saltry.

"Why, no! I'll get a plastic bag to keep them dry, and we'll tie them on the back of your bicycle—or maybe it would be better if I took you back in the car."

"Oh, no, thank you. I shall go on my bicycle. The drizzle has almost stopped, and I enjoy cycling in the rain."

"But it's so windy!"

"It's quite sheltered once you get out of the grounds of the Manor. I must thank you again. . . ."

"Nonsense."

They carried out the plastic bag, and Miss Dell tied it to the carrier of her bicycle. The only thing left out was a gay silk scarf which she had elected to wear. She draped it loosely round her neck.

"It gives a nice touch of colour, don't you think?" she asked.

"It looks very nice. Be careful the ends don't catch in the spokes of the wheel."

"You don't mind giving Mr. Brierley the message?"

"Not at all. Goodbye."

Miss Dell mounted the bicycle and rode off, and Mrs. Saltry walked into the house remembering with shame the self-pity in which she had indulged the day before. Next time she felt sorry for herself, she resolved, she would remember Miss Dell.

She was about to go upstairs when there was a knock, and she opened the door to Cosmo.

"Did you pass Miss Dell?" she asked him. "She left here just a minute or two ago."

Cosmo was looking puzzled. "She passed me, but I don't think she saw me. She was only a few feet away, but she went past me without a glance. She was—"

"She was what?"

"Singing."

"Singing? Miss Dell was singing?"

"Yes. Quite loudly."

"Singing what, for heaven's sake?"

"It sounded like a hymn. Did she seem . . . did you think she acted strangely while she was here?"

"No. But she left your letters, and a message. She wants you to go and warn Lady Laura that she, Miss Dell, saw her outside the Manor this morning, and there was a shadow over her."

Cosmo made a gesture of despair. "Another shadow?"

"Yes. If you go and tell Lady Laura, will she take it seriously?"

"No. She'll be very seriously annoyed."

"Then what will you do—forget it?"

"How can I forget it? I shall have to say something."

"Why? Do you believe something might happen to her?"

"No, I don't. But if I said nothing, and Lady Laura had a fall, or something of that kind, and it came to Miss Dell's knowledge that I had said nothing to warn her, she would hold me responsible. I don't relish going to Lady Laura with a message like that."

"Then go now, this minute."

"Why?"

"Because if there's something you have to do that you don't want to do, always get it over with."

Cosmo smiled. "That's very good advice. I shall go at once."

But he was too late. Lady Laura had decided that the slight drizzle was not sufficient to prevent her from taking her customary drive. She had ordered the governess cart, and at the same moment that Miss Dell left Mrs. Saltry, Lady Laura left the Manor and set off along the lake road towards the bridge. The bicycle and the governess cart were travelling along two roads which converged near the bridge, and if Miss Dell had not been singing a hymn of praise, she would have heard the sound of the pony's hooves. If she had not had her eyes fixed on a vision of herself in Mrs. Saltry's gifts of clothing, she would have seen the approach of the governess cart.

But she saw nothing, and heard nothing. She emerged onto the road leading to the bridge a few moments before Lady Laura reached the junction of the two roads. Cycling briskly, singing loudly, Miss Dell approached the open ground beyond the bridge, and met a strong gust of wind which whipped off the light scarf and carried it away. Miss Dell, unaware of its loss, proceeded on her way. The scarf floated, twisted, swooped and was carried by another gust across the pony's head. It swept past the animal in a moment—but the moment was long enough to make it swerve violently. One of the wheels of the cart struck the root of a tree; the cart overturned and the pony came to a standstill, turning after a while to look without emotion at the figure which lay motionless, still graceful, still elegant, its head in the pretty little hat resting against the trunk of the tree.

It was Banks who, uneasy at the failure of his mistress to return, went out in search of her. It was Banks and his son who, with Cosmo and Hallam, lifted the lifeless form and bore it home. As they laid it on the bed beneath the beautiful canopy, Miss Dell, still singing a hymn of praise, tried on the first of Mrs. Saltry's dresses and found that it fitted perfectly.

CHAPTER

11

It seemed to Nell that every man, woman and child in Rivering attended the funeral. Through the thin, incessant rain, cars drove up and stopped beyond the bridge, and their occupants got out and joined the unending file of mourners who had come on foot. While the vicar read the brief service beside the coffin, Nell could see, beyond the handful who had managed to fit into the tiny chapel, the crowd of soberly clad figures waiting patiently in the rain. Some, she was aware, were the merely curious—but what had brought Daise and Betsy and Charley and Ernie Lauder? What had brought those who, during her lifetime, could not bring themselves to utter her name?

She realized slowly that this was indeed a passing. Here, shortly to be laid beside her forebears, was the last Stapling of Stapling Manor. Here, before the town of Rivering existed, had lived Richard Stapling and his descendants. Through the centuries, the farms ringed by the river had become a hamlet, and the hamlet had grown to a village and the village to a town. The townspeople were here today because their ancestors had been part of the Manor, serving the Staplings in war and in peace, until changing conditions had given them their independence. They had come today in answer to some deep instinct of loyalty, and a desire to see the last Stapling laid to rest.

Miss Dell had come alone, refusing all offers of transport or company. She had walked up the hill, and on her arrival the crowd had made way for her and a respectful murmur had rippled through the waiting groups. The word had spread: it was Miss Dell who had foreseen, foretold the tragedy. Those who had jibed would jibe no longer.

The Moultons were in the chapel, but Mrs. Saltry had remained in Hallam's house. She had watched the steady stream of people walking up through the woods, and then she sat down and let her mind rest for a time on the dead woman, and on the effect her death must have on Nell's future.

She had hot coffee ready when Nell and Hallam and Cosmo, wet and chilled, came in.

"In the kitchen," she told them. "It's warmer in there."

"The vicar's coming in a little while," Nell told her. "And Miss Dell. And the Moultons." She made a restless movement. "Would it be all right if I didn't stay?" she asked Cosmo. "I want to be outside. I want to walk—or something. Couldn't Hallam and I go off somewhere?"

"Drink your coffee first," Mrs. Saltry advised. "You too, Hallam."

When Hallam had finished, he went to the hall and brought Nell her coat.

"Put this on," he said. "Your mac's soaked."

Cosmo opened the front door, and closing it after them, walked slowly back to the kitchen and stood looking at Mrs. Saltry.

"You look washed out," she told him. "Why don't you sit down and give your feet a rest? You've been on them long enough."

He appeared not to have heard.

"All those people," he said wonderingly. "People who had professed to . . . almost to hate her. People who knew her, people who didn't. The old people, who could remember the past—but also the young people who knew her, if they knew her at all, as an autocratic old woman, a survival of the dark ages. People—"

"You can say it just as well sitting down," Mrs. Saltry pointed out. She pushed a stool towards him. "And while you're saying it, remember the packet of trouble she gave you over the years."

"Oh, but one must—"

"—forgive. Forgiving's easy. I can forgive all the time. What's hard is forgetting. Things stick in your mind whether you want them to or not. You're going to stick in mine."

He came back slowly to the present.

"I am?"

"You are. Sit down, I said. That's better. And relax. I'm not going to scare you the way I scared you the other day, talking about taking you on a visit to my house. Nobody's going to take you anywhere—because why? Because this is where you belong. You wouldn't transplant. So you'll stay here, and I'll come visiting, and I'll come pretty often, so's you can't forget me."

"I could never forget you," he said quietly.

She took his empty cup and refilled it.

"I'll see that you don't," she promised.

Nell and Hallam walked round the far side of the lake, away from the dispersing crowd. Without speaking, her hand in Hallam's, Nell took her mind back to the day of her arrival in Rivering and brought it slowly to the moment at which she had stood in the Manor looking down at the calm, dead face of her great-aunt.

"I didn't have long," she said. "Two weeks. Just in time to be—"

"—in at the death. It was a good end. Just a moment of falling, and then nothing more."

"What could have made the pony do that?"

Hallam did not reply. He had his own theory; he had seen, as they bore the body to the Manor, the scarf trailing from the branch of a tree. He had walked back to the scene of the accident, removed it and folded it and carried it to Mrs. Saltry, who had confirmed his guess that Miss Dell had worn it. He had said nothing and would in future say nothing of what he thought; it was mere speculation, and nothing was to be gained by mentioning it.

"Did you expect all those people to come to the funeral?" Nell asked.

"No, but it didn't surprise me. She'll be missed—not for herself, but for what she stood for."

"What did she stand for?"

"Continuity. The old order. History. If you walk back along the line of Staplings, you'll find Henry Tudor standing beside Richard Stapling. If you dug deep into the ancestry of many of the people who stood round the coffin today, you'd find Stapling retainers, men-at-arms, servants of every degree."

She sighed. "How can such a lot happen in just two weeks?"

"It's a long time. Babies arrive in a few hours. Your aunt died within seconds."

"What's to happen about the memorial?"

"It's up to you to decide. My own feeling is that there's no need for one. The direct line's finished, but there's a lot of Stapling blood in you, and there'll be some in our children. As I see it, they're the inheritors."

"That's what I think, too."

"You're not in a state of mind to make any decisions yet. As soon as Corinne goes, you and I are going to pay a visit to my parents. Leave things in Cosmo's hands until we get back. He can look after the business angles and Banks can take care of the Manor. You're going to learn how to be an archaeologist's wife."

"You said they were the same as other men."

"I was wrong. They're a race apart. They need special treatment. And you'll need special treatment until you get your colour back."

"I'm glad I knew her, even though it wasn't for long. But you should be feeling kind of uneasy."

"Why should I?"

"Because Aunt Laura must be finding out something about you."

"Finding out what?"

"What you did with that Bible box."

A Note About the Author

Born and brought up in India, Elizabeth
Cadell was educated in Calcutta, London,
and Darjeeling. She started writing in 1947
and since then has published over two dozen
novels including *The Friendly Air* (1971)
and *Home for the Wedding* (1972). Mrs.
Cadell now lives in Portugal.